Cost of Our Affairs

By Linda R. Herman

Cost of Our Affairs
Consequences: When Love Is Blind
Consequences
Somebody Prayed For Me

And in eBook

Chemistry 101
From Hooker to Housewife
A Time for Love
Lying to Myself
Single Again

Don't miss the next book by your favorite author.
Sign up for Xpress Yourself Publishing's newsletter by visiting
www.XpressYourselfPublishing.org

Cost of Our Affairs

Linda R. Herman

Xpress Yourself Publishing

Xpress Yourself Publishing, LLC
P. O. Box 1615
Upper Marlboro, Maryland 20773

Cost of Our Affairs is a work of fiction. Names, characters, places and incidents are either products of the authors' imagination or are used fictitously. Any resemblance to actual persons, living or dead, business establishments, events or locales is entirely coincidental.

ISBN-10: 0-9779398-7-1
ISBN-13: 978-0-9779398-7-9

Library of Congress Control Number: 2009926710

Printed in the United States of America

Cover Design and Interor Layout by
The Writer's Assistant
www.TheWritersAssistant.com

Visit Xpress Yourself Publishing online:
www.XpressYourselfPublishing.org

Dedication/Acknowledgments

For Ollie M. West
Sunrise: February 14, 1941 – Sunset: January 14, 2006

I dedicate this novel, and all of my works, to a woman who dedicated her life to me, my late grandmother Ollie M. West. God called her home on January 14, 2006, but she is always with me. In every thought that crosses my mind and every word that I utter, she is there. I am eternally grateful for having her as my mother, grandmother, and friend for thirty years.

I'm back! It's only by the grace of God that I can share how thankful and happy I am to announce the release of *Cost of Our Affairs*. Even though *Consequences: When Love Is Blind* was my first published book, *Cost of Our Affairs* is the first novel I began writing in 2005. It was the original Chapter 1 of this novel, which won first place honors in the Black Expressions Fiction Writing Contest in 2005. A lot has changed since then and there are quite a few people I can thank for this. My publisher, Jessica Tilles, first and foremost.

As always, I give thanks to my family and friends for their continued support. You all know who you are and how much you mean to me. Thank you for always being there for me and allowing me to grow, not only as a writer, but as a person, a wife, mother, daughter, sister, niece, aunt, cousin, friend, and so much more. Evette, Seletha, and Lady, thank you for spreading the word about my books to any and every one who would listen,

LOL. It means so much to me. Allyson and Tinisha, you're more like sisters than friends. Thank you for making *Somebody Prayed For Me* a success. So many people have been touched by the stories in the book.

There's a young woman who took the time to help me bring Maya's character to life and I am eternally grateful to you, Amanda. Thank you!

Readers, book clubs, and friends, thank you one and all for choosing books by Linda R. Herman. Without your support, my words would have no audience.

Happy reading! I'm working diligently on my 2011 releases. You'll get a sneak peek into *What's a Wife to Do?* and *In His Father's Arms* at the end of this book.

Until next time, God bless!

Chapter 1

Trees. When her eyes finally fluttered open, all India saw were thick rows of trees. She tried to sit up in her seat, but her head felt like lead. It was pounding and her mouth was dry. She could've sworn a thousand drummers were marching inside her cranium while Sammy himself tap-danced on her brain.

"You awake, Sweetheart?" The sound of his voice made her heart skip a beat, and she prayed that she was dreaming. *Wake up!* She screamed inwardly. *It can't be him.*

He stretched his right arm over and gently caressed her cheek with the backside of his hand. His touch alone made her flesh crawl. She felt like a thousand bees were stinging her.

India managed to roll her head over, coming face to face with her ex-lover, Mario Thomas. He smiled at her lovingly, and her eyes stretched wide in fear, almost popping out of their sockets. India tried to scream, but the sound was trapped inside her taped mouth. She tried to move her arms and feet but realized that they too were duct-taped and despite her weak and sluggish efforts, she couldn't move. Fear caused her heart to race as chills shot down her spine. She wasn't dreaming; it was real.

Turning her head toward the window was a chore, but she couldn't stand the sight of him. She noticed the sun was now peaking over the horizon, signaling daylight's arrival, evidence they'd been traveling for quite some time. She had no idea where they were. At some point, he'd stopped for gas because she remembered having only a quarter of a tank. *Why didn't anyone help me*, she wondered as she tried to remember the details of the previous night.

"Everything's going to be fine, Sharon," he cooed, still caressing her cheek, making her flinch. Bile rose in the back of her throat and she feared choking off her own vomit.

"In a few hours we'll be in our own paradise, far away from those crazy people who think they're your family. Sharon, you'll soon remember our life together, and you won't even think about those people anymore. We'll make a family of our own."

Tears streamed down her face as she listened, the words of a sick man terrified her and waves of nausea turned her stomach in knots. She wanted so badly to slap his hand away from her face. She didn't know how, but she knew she had to get away from him. *Why am I so weak?*

Mario needed help. It was obvious that he'd stopped taking the medication the doctor prescribed after the death of his wife. He fell into an even deeper depression and became delusional. India was terrified of what he may do next if she didn't cooperate. She had to think fast and act even faster. Her only chance of survival was to pretend to be the woman he was convinced she was.

Again, she turned to face him and stared at him intently, silently pleading with him to remove the strip of tape that covered her dry mouth, all the while praying to God for strength. The sight of him was almost unbearable. *Those eyes,* she thought, *why didn't I see the evil before?*

Taking his eyes off the road, Mario smiled sweetly before snatching the tape from her mouth. As if she'd been under water, India gasped for air, heaving loudly as she hungrily inhaled.

"Water. I need water," she pleaded when she finally found her voice.

Mario didn't respond. Focusing on the road, he kept smiling and caressing her cheek as if all was well. Twenty minutes later, he turned into the parking lot of a small gas station.

After parking the car and shutting off the engine, he leaned over and kissed her lips, bringing even more bile to the back of her throat. Knowing her life depended on her every action, India managed a small smile despite the fear and hatred that made it difficult for her to swallow.

"Be right back." Again, he kissed her, opened the driver's door and headed toward the store's entrance.

She took a deep breath and slowly exhaled as her mind raced with thoughts of her escape. *How do I get myself out of this mess?* Her arms and legs were still bound in tape, but looking down, India noticed her purse lying at her feet. If only she could reach it. Her cell phone was in there. She could call for help.

Fueled by determination, she kicked off her shoes and used her bare feet to shuffle the purse around on the floor of her car, spilling its contents. Finally, her phone fell out.

"Thank, God," she exclaimed. Using her toes, she pressed the number three key on the phone's keypad. That was her mother's speed dial.

"Hello? India, baby we're worried about you. Are you okay?"

At the sound of her mother's voice, India's heart filled with hope. "Momma, help! I don't know where I am. Mario's got me!"

She could hear her mother's terror-filled gasp. "Don't hang up the phone, baby. I'm calling the police. Just don't hang up, India."

"Momma, he's coming back," India warned as she saw Mario exiting the store, bottled water in one hand and a bag of food in the other. "Don't say anything, Momma. Don't say a word."

Using her feet once again, she did her best to kick the phone out of sight. Just before he opened the door, she sent the Envy sailing under her seat. She prayed that the call was not disconnected.

Mario opened the bottle of water and pressed it to her dry, cracked lips. She tilted her head back, allowing the cool water to slide down her throat. He opened up the bag and removed a ham and cheese sandwich. She bit it hungrily, gulping it down in a few bites.

"How long do I have to stay taped up, honey?" she asked sweetly.

"Sharon?" His eyes lit up and his face glowed like a full moon.

India nodded affirmatively. If being Sharon Thomas was going to save her life, she'd do her best to be the dead woman.

Mario pulled a knife from his pocket. Her initial reaction was fear, but the pounding in her heart subsided when he used the knife to cut the tape that held her prisoner. Elated, Mario pulled his wife into his arms and kissed her deeply, savoring her sweetness. When she didn't resist, he held her tighter, kissing her even deeper. He wanted to make love to her again, right there in the car, in front of the old gas station, but he knew he had to put more miles between her past and their future.

Despite the nausea she felt, India grinned widely when he finally released her. The throbbing in her head was subsiding and she focused more on her surroundings. The name of the gas station was Stanley's.

"Baby, I've never heard of Stanley's before. Where are we?" she asked as he guided the car out of the parking lot, heading west.

He shrugged his shoulders. "We're somewhere between Alabama and Mississippi but don't worry. Before long, we'll be some place where no one will ever find us. We're just going to keep moving west for now."

India turned away from him and stared out of the window, a true smile on her face this time. She was sure her phone was still open and hoped that her mother and the police were listening. It was only a matter of time before they'd track them down in her car.

She wondered how the hell she got herself into this shit as they passed miles and miles of more trees. Her only hope was being the late Sharon Thomas until the calvary came to her rescue.

Chapter 2

How it all began...

From my office, I watched him. I listened to him as he introduced himself to my colleagues. He was tall and handsome with smooth skin the color of caramel. Wavy curls rested on top of his head. They looked soft and I could almost feel the silky strands as I imagined my hands running through his hair.

Mario Thomas was his name. I'd heard him introduce himself as our new president at Cordelia Bank. We'd all known for quite some time that there would be a replacement for Mr. Charles Winthrop, but I never imagined anyone as fine as Mario Thomas. Unlike Mr. Winthrop, Mario was young, maybe late thirties, and he was a sexy brother.

I saw him turn in my direction, and I heard his footsteps against the hardwood floors as he, accompanied by Vice President Derek Edison, approached my office. I quickly darted my eyes to my computer screen and pretended to be hard at work.

"And this is India Joiner," I heard Derek say. "She's our senior loan officer."

I rose from my chair and walked over to them. "How do you do?" I asked the big boss as I extended my right hand to him.

"India, this is our new president, Mr. Mario Thomas," Derek said as the man took my trembling hand in his. Instead of a simple handshake, he brought my hand to his full lips and kissed it. The heat and moisture from his lips made my knees buckle. I took a quick survey of his left hand and didn't notice a ring. He was single!

"So nice to meet you, Ms. Joiner." He smiled and I was almost blinded by the shine of his pearly white teeth. He was a beautiful creature indeed.

"Excuse me," Teresa, my secretary said, sticking her head into my office. "Mr. Edison, your wife is waiting in your office for you."

"If you two will excuse me. I owe my beautiful wife a lunch date." That said Derek was gone and I was left standing face to face with Mario Thomas. I silently begged my weakened legs not to fail me and send me crashing to the floor.

The smell of his Burberry cologne was driving me crazy. He had to know I was uncomfortable. Like a hyperactive child, I couldn't stand still. I shuffled my feet nervously, folded and unfolded my arms across my chest, and smiled awkwardly. You wouldn't have known I'd been exposed to fine men before by the way I was acting.

"Well, this is a beautiful office you have here," he complimented as he admired the paintings on my wall. I admired his swagger as he made his way over to my window. "And this view is magnificent. I'm jealous." *The view ain't bad from where I'm standing either. What am I thinking? Back to being a professional,* I chastised.

The view *from my office* was astounding. It was the reason I, as the senior loan officer, had chosen this office. From my window, I could see all of downtown Cordele in its glorified beauty. I admired the exquisite waterfall that sat in the middle of the park and the busy city streets filled with cars and people as they traveled back and forth to their daily destinations. But, despite the paintings and the gorgeous view, my office was nothing compared to the president's grand office.

"Are you kidding me?" I tried but couldn't stifle the laughter. My little corner of the world couldn't compete with his slice of heaven. Sure, I was moving on up but hell, he was already there.

"I've seen your office. It's big enough for you, the wife, and kids to live in." *Yes, I went there.* I didn't see a ring, but I had to confirm his status.

Smiling, he held up his left hand. There wasn't a ring, but there was an imprint. Even if he wasn't married he had been and not very long ago.

"No wife and kids. It's just me." He didn't offer any further explanation and even though I was dying to know more, I didn't press.

"Well, even so, your office is beautiful. You have the finest mahogany furniture in there and it's professionally decorated. And let's not even mention that big, luxurious bathroom that's equipped with a Jacuzzi tub." I wasn't sure if he knew it but all that luxury had gotten Mr. Winthrop fired.

"Have you spent a lot of time up there?" he asked, pointing upstairs. His office, as well as Derek's, was on the third floor. Both were huge. They were the only two offices on the entire floor.

"Oh no," I answered quickly. I wasn't the one who had spent a lot of time in there with Mr. Winthrop. Cecily, a former teller, had been his mistress. She had been the one who told all of us about the beautiful office and her affair with Charles, as she called him. Her constant bragging soon got back to his wife and corporate office. Shortly after that, Cecily and Charles were both without a job. Charles was also without his wife of thirty something odd years. "I was up there once when I interviewed for a job here five years ago, and again when I was promoted to my current position a year ago. But, I've heard a lot." I added with a smile.

"Can't believe all that you hear. Why don't you come up and have lunch with me sometimes?" *Is he flirting with me? I do believe so!*

Despite his intense stare and seductive smile, I didn't answer. Changing the subject, he asked me about the paintings in my office. "Where did you find such lovely paintings? Did they come with the office?"

"No." I then cleared my throat. "My husband painted them." I should have told him I was married a lot sooner. "I tell him all the time that he should be getting paid for his work, but he won't market his paintings."

"That's a shame," Mario said as his eyes lingered on the painting of the exquisite waterfalls. "These are good. I would definitely buy some for my home and office."

I nodded in agreement, and we found ourselves standing in an awkward silence that blanketed the entire office.

"Well," he finally said with a devious smile forming in the corner of those luscious lips.

"Well," I repeated nervously as I made my way back to my desk. "I have a lot of work to do." I sat back down and pretended to be engrossed with the numbers on my computer screen. Truth was, if I'd spent five more minutes with that man I would've literally thrown myself at him.

"The lunch offer is good. Just say when," he said as he threw up his right hand to signal goodbye.

"Thank you," I replied without looking up at him. "Please close the door behind you."

When I heard the click of the door closing, I rolled backward in my chair and exhaled. *Damn!* I closed my eyes and leaned back in the chair, fantasizing about Mario taking me on my office desk. I ran my hands through his hair as he devoured me. The tips of my manicured nails gently scratched his back as he entered me while staring into my eyes. I smelled my sweet nectar on his breath with every raspy exhale.

"Excuse me," Teresa interrupted. She probably knocked, but I couldn't hear it for the pounding in my chest. "Will you be ordering in today?"

I looked up at the clock and realized it was past noon. Teresa and I normally ordered take out and worked through lunch. Rarely did I leave the office, even if Teresa decided to go out for lunch. Today, I had no choice but to leave though.

"I'm going home for lunch, Teresa. What about you?"

"I'm going to grab a bite and eat in the park," she answered.

"Very well then."

That said I grabbed my purse and headed toward the elevator. I had to hurry and get home. Mario's presence alone made me cum and my panties were soaking wet. I couldn't imagine what would happen if I ever took him up on his offer to have lunch in his office. We would both probably burst into flames and spontaneously combust.

Chapter 3

Mario went on about the task of getting acquainted with the staff of Cordelia Bank but through all the smiles, handshaking, come-ons, and ass kissing, he couldn't shake thoughts of India Joiner from his mind.

Sure, she was married but that was a minor obstacle. Mario saw how her eyes roamed over him, checking out his left hand to see if he was married. If she were happily married, she wouldn't have cared one way or the other if he had a significant other.

The woman was fine, too fine to be true. She reminded him so much of Sharon, the only woman who'd ever managed to tame him, a well-known ladies' man. But now, in his late thirties, with no one to go home to, being a ladies' man wasn't what Mario desired. He wanted India, not someone like her, he wanted her, and he was determined to have her.

In his office, he reclined in his leather, executive style chair behind his mahogany desk. His secretary, Emily, buzzed him. "You have a call on line one. It's a Dr. Martin," she announced.

His blood boiled as he snatched the phone from its base. How many times had he told this man to stop calling him? "Mario Thomas," he barked into the mouthpiece.

"Mr. Thomas, it's Dr. Martin." The man paused briefly, as if he were waiting for a more formal greeting from Mario. When he didn't receive one, he continued, "I'm just calling to check on you, Mr. Thomas. I was hoping you were ready to start our weekly sessions again."

Mario wanted to reach through the phone and grab the doctor's scrawny neck. He wanted to choke the life out of him. He'd told the man many times that he was healed. He didn't need a shrink or any medication because he wasn't crazy. Lonely, yes, but crazy, hell no.

"Doc, I told you once, twice, and too many times already, that I don't need your services. I'm dealing with my loss," he spoke as calmly as possible. "I would strongly suggest that you stop calling me before I take legal action."

Before the doctor could respond, he heard the sound of a dial tone in his right ear. He looked at the phone's receiver before placing it back in its cradle. Shaking his head, Dr. Martin reclined in his chair, clicking his ink pen.

"Mario Thomas is a very sick man. God have mercy on the next woman he obsesses over," the doctor said aloud before adding, "and anyone who tries to stop him."

Chapter 4

After a long day at work, I came home to more work. I would have loved to just fill my garden tub with water and bubbles and relax. God knows I needed it after a stressful day at the bank. Just because I was a sister and the senior loan officer, people expected me to be able to approve loans no matter how risky they were. They didn't understand that I had a higher authority to answer to. There were some loans that I just could not approve. By the end of the day, I was called more house niggers and black bitches than I cared to count.

But, that bubble bath would just have to wait. First, there was dusting, vacuuming, sweeping, washing, drying, and folding of clothes to be done. The kids had homework and then there was dinner to be cooked before Antoine came home at seven-thirty. It was already five o'clock.

"How was school?" I asked the kids as they climbed into my baby blue BMW. I was picking them up from my mother's, as usual. They rode the bus to her home daily because I was not out of the office until after four o'clock. That's on a good day. Today, I was lucky to get out before five o'clock.

"I made an A on my math test," my nine-year-old son, Trey, replied. He was an honor roll student and I was so proud of him.

I waited on a reply from Ariel, my eight-year-old stepdaughter. When she didn't respond, I addressed her directly. "What about you, Ariel? How was your day?"

"My mommy said I don't have to talk to you. You're not my real momma, and she don't like you, so I don't like you."

I felt my blood boil as my eyes automatically rolled on cue. *Calm down, India. This is nothing new.* Ariel's mother, Rachel, had been teaching this child how to disrespect me for over a year now. That's how long Ariel had been living with us. Antoine was granted custody of her when Rachel was proven to be the unfit mother everyone always knew she was.

After counting to a zillion and mumbling a few, *woo-sahs*, I calmly addressed Ariel. "You may not like me, but you will respect me," I told her firmly. "I asked you a question, and I expect an answer."

She was silent for a few seconds but finally mumbled, "Fine."

Through the rearview mirror, I saw her eyes rolling and I sent up a quick prayer to God. *Father God, please guide my hands so I don't reach back and snatch this child.* The last thing I needed was to lose control of my temper and my car.

I was at the point of not knowing what to do in this situation. I loved Ariel and I tried my best to treat her no differently than I treated my own child. It was getting harder by the day having to deal with her attitude. I knew it was Rachel who was to blame, but just as Rachel taught her hate, Antoine and I taught Ariel love. She chose to listen only to her mother's venom.

As I guided the car into the carport, I thanked God for answering my prayer and allowing us to get home safely. Inside, I got the kids started on their homework and I started dinner after sorting laundry. It was Wednesday, my weekday washday. There was not a whole lot to wash, so I didn't hesitate to get the task under way and out of the way. By keeping busy, I hoped to dismiss thoughts of Mario, which was a far cry from easy.

The house wasn't dirty, so it didn't take long to go through my daily routine of dusting, vacuuming, and sweeping. I cleaned the downstairs half bath first. When I was finished downstairs, I washed my hands and headed back to the kitchen to stir the beans that were cooking, checked on the chicken in the oven, and started mixing the cornbread batter. I would do the rice last. It only took ten minutes to boil that in the microwave. The upstairs cleaning of the bathrooms could wait 'til after dinner.

"How's the homework coming?" I asked the kids as I placed the cornbread in the oven. I figured I might as well go ahead and put the rice in the microwave now. If the kids didn't need any help, I would have time to clean the bathrooms upstairs before dinner after all.

"I'm almost done," my son answered. Again, Ariel ignored me. She just sat there holding her pencil in her hand. Her papers were still blank.

"Ariel, you need any help?" I offered after I put the rice in the microwave.

"No. I don't want you to help me. I'll ask my daddy to help me." I didn't argue with her. I didn't even have the strength. She was pressing real hard on my last good nerve.

"Suit yourself." I hurried upstairs to clean our bathroom and theirs.

One of these days, I thought as I scrubbed their tub. I wasn't sure how much more I could take and talking to Antoine about the situation never seemed to help matters. No matter how calmly

I approached him, we always ended up in a shouting match, both determined to be heard but surely smart enough to know that our heartfelt words were dying in mid-air as they crashed into each other. As much as I loved him and Ariel, I often wondered if the hell I went through, trying to be a good wife and stepmother, was worth it.

I came back downstairs in time to get the bread out of the oven before it burned. I smiled when I saw the golden brown bread. It was perfect.

"You two set the table," I instructed Trey and Ariel. "I've got to get this last load of clothes out of the dryer."

I headed outside to our carport where our washer and dryer were located. I took the warm clothes out of the dryer and headed back inside to fold them and put them away. Antoine was due home in fifteen minutes.

I noticed Ariel sitting in the same spot when I returned. That little heifer hadn't moved an inch! Trey was busy setting the table as I'd asked them both to do. Again I asked myself, *is it worth it?*

"Ariel, why aren't you helping set the table?" I was trying to be calm, but she was wearing my patience thin. I was two seconds off her rear end.

"I didn't want to. My mommy said if I don't want to, then I don't have to."

My mommy said this; my mommy said that. I was so sick of hearing that bullshit every single day. All the anger I'd been holding back came to the surface and I went off.

"Your mommy doesn't live in this house! Around here you do what I tell you to do. I won't put up with any more of your disrespect, Ariel."

Again, she rolled her eyes at me and I gave serious thought to snatching her out her chair and shaking the hell out of her. *That's what the devil wants me to do*, I reasoned, taking a deep breath. The more I looked at her, the more I leaned toward Satan's plan. I had to maintain so I closed my eyes. *Ten, nine, eight, seven...*

My eyes opened at the sound of the carport door closing. In walked my husband looking as if he'd had another tiring, hard day. He worked in the production plant at Pepsi and they had been working overtime for months now. He had to be in at seven and didn't leave work until after seven. Sometimes they even worked on Saturdays.

"Daddy! Daddy! India's going to hit me!" His daughter abandoned her seat and raced to him, falling into his arms, falsely seeking protection from me, the evil stepmother.

"I was trying to do my homework and she wanted me to set the table. When I didn't, she started yelling at me." She was in tears now. That little heifer was a damn good actress.

"What's going on today, India?" Antoine glared at me as he rubbed Ariel's back, comforting her and no doubt ready to condemn me.

This little scene happened at least once a week, sometimes more. It always started with me telling her something to do, her disobeying and disrespecting me, and then Antoine and me having it out when she claimed I was mistreating her in one way or another.

I wasn't feeling like their drama today. Without answering, I continued with my task of folding laundry. Once done, I took the basket of folded clothes and left the kitchen. When I came back downstairs, they had started dinner without me. I went through the trouble of preparing the meal, but they didn't even have the decency to wait on me before they dug in.

Ariel was chattering non-stop to Antoine about her day at school. Trey ate his food while quietly reading a book. Not caring to join them at the family table, I fixed my plate and took a seat at the island. There was no way I could stand to be in the presence of Ariel and Antoine in that moment. I was too angry.

"I don't know how to do this math," Ariel told her father. "Will you help me?" She acted as if I didn't offer to help her at all. Steam had to be rising from both my ears. I was so pissed that I could have spit fire like a mystical dragon.

"I'll help you as soon as I take my shower," he assured his little princess before cutting his eyes toward me. "Can we talk upstairs?"

Hmmp, am I supposed to be scared? I was not going anywhere until I finished eating, loading the dishwater, and putting the food away. With much attitude, I replied, "Whatever."

Upstairs we did what we had been doing for the past six months or longer. We argued. He accused me of not being there for Ariel the way I was for Trey. I argued that I tried but Ariel, thanks to Rachel, wouldn't let me be there for her. That wasn't good enough for him though.

"You're the adult, India. Act like it."

And that's the way our fights about Ariel always ended. I was reprimanded and reminded that I was the adult and then like a child, I was told to act like it. It didn't matter that Rachel was the true antagonist in this situation. He always took his frustrations out on me.

What really hurt was knowing that Ariel and I were once close. When she first came to live with us, she was a sweet and obedient little girl. We didn't have arguments; we had fun together. But as soon as Rachel saw how well we were getting along, she turned Ariel against me, convincing her that I didn't care for her. Somehow, she made that child believe that I was the enemy. Things hadn't been the same since even though I'd love for them to be.

At the end of yet another disastrous day, I tucked my son in, and took that long, hot, steamy bubble bath I had been dreaming about since lunch. I closed my eyes, allowing the water to wash my stress away. As soon as I was relaxed and my mind was off Antoine, Ariel, and that bitch Rachel, thoughts of Mario tiptoed into my psyche. I welcomed his presence.

I slid deeper into the warm bubbles as I imagined myself on top of him in his office, on his desk. I slid up and down his steel pole as he squeezed my ass cheeks. The harder he squeezed the faster I rode him, grinding my flesh into his faster, deeper, and harder. His expression changed and I knew he was about to cum. He moved his hands to my shoulders and pressed down. Together we…

"India, when are you coming to bed?"

Damn him! I was almost there! Effortlessly, I rolled my eyes. Not like he had a clue but he could've waited until I came. *It takes a special kind of man to ruin a fantasy.*

"I don't wanna fight and I'm sorry," he apologized when I didn't respond. *That you are,* I silently agreed.

I didn't give a damn about him being sorry. I was more upset with him for interrupting my fantasy than I was about his words earlier. I'd grown accustomed to him siding with the little princess. We went through the same song and dance every time. We fought and then he wanted to make up. The only thing different about today was that I had another option. I could say to hell with all this stress and meet Mario in his office for lunch and *dessert*. If things didn't improve at home that's just what I planned on doing.

Chapter 5

Antoine felt bad for verbally attacking India. He knew that she loved Ariel, but he was so tired of all the bickering between his wife and his daughter. Really, when was the shit going to end? Ariel was just a child, he expected her to behave as such, but India was a grown ass woman who knew that Ariel was not the culprit. Rachel was the evil force driving Ariel, and India was smart enough to see that instead of feeding into it, making matters worse. He was left in the middle every single time, and how does a man choose sides between his wife and his daughter?

But he didn't want to think about any of that drama. Antoine just wanted to bury his head between his wife's thighs and feed off her for the next half hour. He'd make it up to her by using his tongue to apologize and bring her to orgasm. She always liked that, and he couldn't deny that he liked the taste of her sweet juices on his tongue.

India emerged from the bathroom, wearing not a stitch of clothing. He licked his lips, eyeing her pretty kitty, ready for a pussy galore feast. She didn't return his enthusiasm. Instead of a warm smile, she rolled her eyes, and sighed in disgust.

"I'm sick of this same shit, Antoine. You think fucking is going to solve our problems?"

Here she go, he thought. All he wanted to do was make love to his wife, hold her in his arms, and sleep through the night, without another fight. India had a different agenda though, one that left him wondering if he would be so lucky to fall asleep with her juices on his tongue after all.

Antoine gently pulled his wife down on their bed, massaging her shoulders, and planting soft kisses on her neck. She smelled so good, just like green apples and vanilla.

"I'm sorry, baby," he murmured while gently nibbling at her earlobe. "I love you, and I know you love Ariel. I don't want Rachel to ruin this moment, India."

India turned to face her husband, gently pushing him away, so that they were staring eye to eye. "I don't want her to ruin our marriage, Antoine. It's about more than just a moment. I…"

Antoine pulled her face into his and parted her lips with his tongue. He pulled her tongue into his mouth and sucked it passionately. Reluctantly, she returned the passion and allowed him to have his way with her. He sucked on her neck, leaving his love bites there and between her breasts, before planting more between her thighs. Tears fell from her eyes as he licked, sucked, and nibbled on her clit, making her orgasm repeatedly for nearly an hour.

"I love you. I won't let Rachel ruin that for us, I promise," he proclaimed as he entered her. A deep moan escaped his throat as his penis expanded, filling her completely. "I don't wanna lose you. I never wanna lose you," he declared before planting his seeds.

He held her in his arms long after their bodies stopped trembling, wanting to believe that things would be fine, yet getting an eerie feeling that she was slowly slipping away from him. *Just what the hell can I do about that?*

Chapter 6

Things went from bad to what the hell in no time. The weekly fights with Antoine and me became daily fights. Ariel's behavior worsened with every passing day, and of course Antoine couldn't see the forest for the trees.

Our latest fight occurred while visiting Antoine's family on a Sunday afternoon. We spent every Sunday after church services visiting with my mother, Cassandra Jordan, and then with his mother, Beverly Joiner.

I was inside watching television while Antoine and his mother ate in the small kitchen. Antoine's sisters, Annette and Lisa were outside with Rachel. Rachel and Annette had been best friends since school, and Rachel was a regular guest at the Joiner home. Like Rachel, Annette and Lisa were nothing but trouble.

Ariel and the other kids were outside playing before Ariel came inside and told me, "My mommy said you're a bitch! And Auntee Lisa and Auntee Annette said my mommy and Daddy are going to get married, bitch!"

"What did you just say?" I was enraged now. I had put up with a lot but no one; child or adult was going to get away with calling me a bitch.

Antoine ran into the living room when he heard my elevated voice. "What's going on? Why are you yelling at her?" Of course, Ariel was in tears at that point. Her mother and aunts burst through the front door cussing, swearing, and threatening me. I wasn't afraid though. It was me against the fucking world and I wanted to take all three of them on.

"Ariel came in here and called me a bitch!" I told my husband, my voice still a few octaves about the norm. "And she told me you're the one who called me a bitch, you fat bitch!" I got in Rachel's face. She was only five feet tall but weighed well over two-hundred and fifty pounds. Her size didn't intimidate me for a second. I was ready for what the hell ever.

Rachel didn't open her mouth to say a word. I moved on to my wicked sister in laws. "And I hear you two are telling her that Rachel and Antoine are getting married, huh?"

They both smacked their lips and rolled their eyes, but there was no more cussing and swearing. I'd fought with Annette once before and I think I left an impression on her ass that soap and water wouldn't wash away. They didn't want none. It was so quiet in that room, a farting fly could have been identified.

"If you know Rachel's the one telling her all this, why are you yelling at Ariel? She's only eight years old, India!" Now Antoine was yelling at me. He didn't yell at his baby's momma who had started all the drama. He yelled at me while she and his sisters stood by with victorious smirks on their faces.

The other kids were now inside as well. All eyes were on me, and I was trying my best not to cry. I was hurt, but more than anything I was pissed off. *How dare he yell at me and talk down to me instead of handling his business with his daughter and her no good mammy! And what about his sisters, the other drama queens?* Again, I asked myself, *is it worth it?*

"I'm going home," I said to him. I didn't care if he came with me or if he came at all. Turning to my son, I said, "Trey, let's go." I took him by the hand and headed out the house.

"India, Baby, don't leave," Ms. Beverly called behind me. I continued out the door without answering. I heard her say to Rachel, "You should be ashamed of yourself for using your own child to hurt her stepmother. India is good to Ariel. She loves her."

I don't know what she said after that because I jumped in the Escalade, fired up the engine, and started backing out of the driveway.

Antoine flagged me down just as the Escalade's tires hit the edge of the highway. He and Ariel climbed in with us but not a word was spoken. There were no apologies and no further explanations. We rode home in total silence. Not even the kids breathed a word.

I stopped in our circular driveway in front of our home instead of pulling into the garage. "You're not coming in?" Antoine asked. In response, I shook my head no. I didn't offer him anything more. At that point, I didn't feel him worthy of an explanation after the way he'd humiliated me at his mother's, in front of everyone.

"India, I know things have been rough between us, but I know it's going to get better. You just got to remember that Ariel is…"

"…only a child. I'm the adult and I should act like it," I finished for him. "It's just that simple to you isn't it? My son's not constantly and repeatedly disrespecting you. He doesn't cuss you or disobey you. And if he did, I'd handle that." Even though I had tried not to, I was now crying.

"Baby, let's just go inside and talk this out," he pleaded with me as he wiped the tears away from my cheeks. I slapped his hands away. I didn't wanna talk. I wanted to get far away from him and Ariel, his evil little princess.

"Daddy, can we get out?" Ariel asked from the back seat, unaffected by my tears. He told her yes and both kids climbed out of the truck and stood by the front door.

"Come on, India. You know Rachel is behind this. Are you going to let her come between us?"

I couldn't believe he asked me that question. He was the one letting her destroy his child and our family. Ariel, thanks to Rachel, had gone from an A student to a below average student, bringing home D's and F's. She didn't want to sing in the church choir anymore or do the praise dances. Nothing good held her interest, only evil.

"That's a question you need to answer. Are *you* going to let her come between us? You knew today that she was behind Ariel calling me a bitch, but you didn't go off on her. You went off on me in front of her and your instigating ass sisters. And you didn't get on to Ariel either. She's a child but she knows better than to call me a bitch."

"She's only eight," he repeated like a broken record. That infuriated me to the point of no return.

Before he could say anything else I told him to get out. I didn't want to hear another word he had to say. When it came to Ariel, he saw no wrong. *Maybe he and Rachel should get back together and get married. They'd be doing me a favor.*

After standing in the open car door for what seemed an eternity, he reluctantly closed it, and I immediately pulled off.

I retrieved my phone from my purse and dialed my best friend. Maya answered on the second ring. "What's up?"

"More drama." I sighed deeply. "Can I come over, Maya? I really need you right now, Sis."

"You know I'm here for you."

That's just what I needed. I needed someone to be there for me. I thanked God for my friend as I drove toward her suburban home.

Chapter 7

"I understand that she's just a child, but I wanted to floor her little ass for calling *me* a bitch."

Maya listened intently as her best friend ranted about the latest dramatic episode between her and Ariel. "India! You can't go around hitting eight year olds!" Maya laughed, knowing that India was only blowing off steam. She knew that Ariel's behavior was causing major problems between India and her husband, Antoine. Maya also knew, without doubt, that India loved Antoine with all of her heart. She didn't want to lose him, which was why she tried so hard to make things better with Ariel.

"Now, I do agree that she was way out of line and even at eight years old she knows better, but I wouldn't have hit her. I would have told her that she was wrong to say such things." Maya saw India sigh deeply and roll her eyes. "Then I would have knocked the hell out of Rachel! Now, that's the bitch that should have been floored."

That comment drew laughter from India, and Maya felt better. She knew her friend needed a good laugh. They had been close for what felt like an eternity. India was like a sister to Maya, who was an only child.

"True. True," India agreed. "Antoine never says anything to Ariel about her behavior toward me. I'm so tired of this bullshit." Her voice cracked as emotions took over.

"He's wrong. Now, when the boys get out of line, Tony doesn't hesitate to put those lil' butts in check." Maya and Tony were the proud parents of three. Terrell, Tyriek, and Toddrick knew not to get out of line because like Maya said, Tony would line them up like little soldiers.

"I can't stand to whip them, but Tony will. He says either we discipline them now or the white man will damn near kill them later when they're locked up."

India nodded in agreement as she topped off the rest of her Alize. She drank two glasses and that was it. India didn't want to get herself killed nor did she intend to kill anyone else on her way home.

"Trey knows better. He doesn't mouth off at adults. Momma tore his behind up one day in the supermarket when he bumped into an old lady and didn't want to apologize. Since then, we have no problems out of Trey." India's eyes always lit up when she spoke of her only birth child.

The two women talked a few more hours about how their parents disciplined them, love, life, and basically nothing at all. They loved being in each other's company being their time together was limited. Both women were married with kids. India worked full time at the bank, and even though Maya didn't work full time she sold Mary Kay products and was always hosting cosmetic parties. She enjoyed the work, but she longed to work full time outside of the home even though Tony didn't want her to.

"So, what are you going to do about Ariel and Antoine?" Maya asked her best friend.

"What can I do?" India wiped down the coffee table. "I love my husband and I love Ariel. I don't know what to do." Thoughts, lewd thoughts, of Mario were dancing around in her head. It had been over a month since his lunch invitation, but still he reminded her at least once a week that the offer was still good. She was growing weaker as she and Antoine continued to fight daily.

"The best thing to do is sit Antoine down and talk to him. Let him know just how you feel and just what you plan to do if things don't change," Maya advised.

What am I planning to do if things don't change? She couldn't tell him that she was planning to have lunch and more with her boss.

"He doesn't want to hear about my plan B," she said with a devious smile.

"Are you still lusting after that boss of yours?" Maya asked when she noticed the naughty girl smile on India's beautiful face. She'd had the pleasure of seeing Mario Thomas, and yes, he was fine. That she couldn't deny. But, Maya knew that Mario was not the answer to India's marital problems. If anything he would make matters worse. A man that fine could make any woman break her marital vows.

"That's definitely not the answer," Ms. Goody Two Shoes continued. "If anything, getting involved with him is only going to add to your problems."

They didn't discuss Mario any further. They finished the cleaning from their wine and cheese party, hugged each other, and said their goodbyes. India's mind was made up anyway. She was going to accept Mario's lunch invitation. It was a risk she'd take. And even though she didn't share her decision with Maya, as her best friend, Maya already knew India was about to make a decision that would change the course of her life forever. The only thing she could do was be there to catch India, praying the fall wouldn't be too hard.

Chapter 8

"So, how long have you been married?"

I was in Mario's office having lunch, with no regrets. He'd ordered take out from El Metate, my favorite Mexican restaurant.

I looked at the rock on my left hand and smiled. Even though I'd reached that point of being fed up, I still loved Antoine. "Six years."

Antoine and I had known each other for awhile before we started dating, but back then my heart belonged to Trey's deadbeat father, Terrance. It wasn't until after finally letting that relationship go that Antoine and I became romantically involved. By that time he and Rachel had called it quits and she wasn't allowing him to have any visitation with Ariel.

"That's a long time," he said, wiping salsa from his lips. I wanted to lick it off. "Your husband is a lucky man."

Too bad he doesn't know that. "What about you? You ever been married?"

He was quiet for a minute. I noticed a sad look in his green eyes. When he finally replied his voice was low. "I was. My wife, Sharon, died of cancer a year ago."

I wanted to go to him and wrap my arms around him. It had to be a terrible thing to lose a spouse. My mother nearly lost it when Daddy Jordan, my stepfather, was killed in a tragic car accident just a few yards away from their driveway. She heard the loud crash and caught only the taillights of the drunk driver's car as he or she sped away.

She rushed to her husband's aid, but he died right there, in her arms. I wondered if Mario's wife had quietly slipped away in his arms.

"I'm sorry to hear that," I managed to say, tears stinging my eyes.

"Thanks." His voice was stronger now and he offered me a smile. "We never had kids. She always wanted to, but we couldn't for whatever reason. It sure would have been nice to have a daughter or a son though." I could tell by his facial expression that he missed her and that he regretted not having a child, a part of her that was still here with him. He must have been so lonely. As much as Antoine and I fought, I could not imagine my life without him. My life without him and our kids would be no life at all.

"You and your husband have any kids?" he asked after a few moments of silence.

"I have a son from a previous relationship and my husband has a daughter from a previous relationship. She's been living with us for about a year or so now." *One year, two months, three weeks, four days, and some odd hours to be exact, but who's counting?* "We don't have any kids together. Not yet."

"How's your relationship with your stepdaughter?" He must have sensed some tension in my voice. It was hard to disguise it as things spun more and more out of control between Antoine, Ariel, and me. The tension at home was so thick it required a chainsaw to cut through it.

"Not great," I admitted. "She's eight going on thirty, and her mother has put the idea in her head that she doesn't have to obey or respect me."

"How does this affect the relationship between your husband and you?" Now he was getting all up in my business. I gave him a curt smile. *Enough already,* my body language screamed as I shifted uncomfortably. He held up his hands, laughed, and said, "I don't mean to pry."

"We have our good days. Then we have those not so good days. Let's just leave it at that." I did not agree to meet him to talk about Antoine and me. And I surely didn't want to discuss Rachel's tactics or Ariel's behavior. He was not my therapist. I wouldn't have minded lying down on his couch, but it surely had nothing to do with counseling.

"Well, anytime you need to talk, I'm a great listener."

I thanked him for the genuine offer, but I knew it was best for me not to start confiding in him. That's what happened with Derek, the vice president and his former secretary, the very crazy Tia Jeffries. She got him to feel all sorry for her because she was being abused by her boyfriend, and then he started confiding in her about his problems with Elise. Few people knew it but that led to an affair and from that affair a child, Terrica, was born. Elise didn't know about the child for years but Tia, God rest her crazy ass soul, was killed by an ex boyfriend. Now, Derek and Elise were raising Terrica along with their other kids. The last thing I needed was some *other baby daddy* drama. I worked too hard to lose my marriage and my job over drama.

We finished our meal. When I looked at the clock, it was only twelve-thirty, and I still had thirty minutes left on my lunch break. Mario's eyes followed mine to the wall.

"You're not going to rush out of here, are you?" he asked when I started cleaning up my mess.

I had no intentions of hanging around. His office could get me in the same kind of trouble that it got Mr. Winthrop and Cecily in. Well, the trouble they got themselves into. The office didn't make them do what they did, but if those walls could talk—the things they'd say.

"Well, I was thinking of taking a stroll in the park. I need to burn off some calories." It was an excuse to get out of his office. The more I thought about it though, the more I knew I would enjoy a breath of fresh air.

"I'll join you." He gathered his debris and combined it with mine before tossing it into the trash receptacle.

Together we walked across the busy intersection to beautiful Watermelon Park. The park was named after Cordele's prestigious national title, The Watermelon Capital of the World. All the park benches were painted the color of watermelons, green and red with black seeds. They looked delicious.

It was a warm day in early April. I was wearing a navy pant suit with a sheer light blue blouse underneath a long sleeved jacket. Mario was wearing a navy Armani suit with a light blue shirt underneath. If one didn't know any better they would think we coordinated our wardrobes. We looked like the perfect couple. Our attractive faces belonged on the cover of *Essence* or *Jet*.

It was hot and humid, so we stood near the waterfall and watched the water glisten as the sun's rays beamed down. Underneath the trees and near the water, we found a cooler place. It was refuge from the sun.

"I never realized how beautiful it is out here," Mario commented as he looked around the park. "Maybe next time we can have our lunch out here by the waterfall."

Next time? My, my, my, is he cocky and confident. Who told him there'd be a next time? "Did I say we were having lunch together again?" I had to at least pretend to play hard to get. Truth was he touched my spirit the moment he spoke of his late wife. I saw more than his pretty boy appeal and those mysterious green eyes. I actually saw the softer side that men usually bury beneath their tough exterior.

"I was hoping you'd let me slide by with that one." His smile was bright enough to light up the universe on its darkest of days.

He was putting on all the charm and I was falling for it. He was so damn good looking and I loved that he was mature and intelligent. I loved the sensitive side I saw in him when he spoke about his late wife. I wanted him. I wanted him badly. But there had to be rules if we were going to have an affair. I was a woman fed up, yes, but still a married woman very much in love with her husband.

"I really don't think we should do this again." His face grew long but I wasn't done speaking. "There are too many eyes and ears. If we're going to see each other, we have to be discreet." That brought a smile back to his face. "We have to see each other outside of the bank and no one, and I do mean no one, can know about this. I'm a married woman and even though my husband and I are having problems, I love him. I'm not going to leave him, and I'm not trying to get caught up and have him leave me. Do we have an understanding?"

Like an eager child, he nodded affirmatively. "I understand fully. When can we get together?"

Though I was calling the shots and playing it cool, I was aching for his touch. I couldn't wait to be alone with him, away from the bank and far away from all the drama that had invaded my home. I needed an escape from my own reality, even if it was nothing but a mere few hours with a man I barely knew. There was a fire burning within me that only he could extinguish. I wanted him to take me to a place that Antoine no longer could-ecstasy.

"Friday, at The Plaza." *Hell, today is Tuesday and I am going to be miserable until then.*

"Friday it is." The smile upon his luscious lips made my knees buckle. *The things I want to do to this man.*

Chapter 9

Finally! Things were progressing with India and like an eager child, Mario agreed to her terms. He could be discreet. He'd agree to damn near anything just to be near her.

He walked her back to her office, ignoring the questioning stare from her secretary. He watched her disappear into the office, smiling before closing the door. He wanted nothing more than to strip her bare, lay her on the desk, and plant soft kisses all over her nude body. But she made it clear that no one could know, so he headed to the third floor to his office, hell bent on honoring her wishes.

Mario couldn't believe that God had answered his prayers. He brought Sharon back to him. India walked like her, talked like her, and she even smelled like his beloved Sharon. She had the same beautiful eyes, and Mario couldn't wait to confirm that she even tasted like the love of his life.

Cancer took Sharon away from him a year ago despite all the money he spent on chemo and experimental treatment. She still died in his arms, her eyes filled with tears. His own tears fell onto her lifeless body as he held her, rocking her in his arms, long after her breathing ceased.

But now he had a second chance, and nothing or no one was going to stand between him and the love of his life. *India's* husband best prepare for the fight of his life because Mario was never going to let his sweet love leave him, not ever again.

Chapter 10

"India, are you listening to yourself?"

If she could have, Maya would have reached through the phone and shook some sense into her best friend. She couldn't believe that girl was going out with Mario Thomas.

"Did you happen to forget that you're a married woman?" Maya asked, fuming.

India was in her office, behind closed doors. She was turned facing her window, watching the waterfall. She guessed Maya would have a negative reaction to her news, but she had no idea her best friend would be this angry.

"Maya, calm down. You act like I just killed somebody. Dang!" She was really working India's nerves. Men had affairs all the damn times, and India would bet her last dollar that their boys weren't bitching to them about it the way Maya was preaching to her. Besides, she wasn't convinced that anything would come of her evening with Mario. It wasn't as if she didn't love Antoine, because she did. Until now, she never entertained the thought of being with another man and as physically attracted as she was to Mario, she still wasn't convinced she was going to sleep with him. Her body screamed yes, but her conscience repeatedly warned against it. She didn't know what to do.

Maya sighed deeply, in a feeble attempt to calm herself. India had her blood pressure rising by the second. "If you go through with this, think about at what cost. What will be the cost of this affair, India? Is it worth it to lose your husband, your family, and your self respect all for a man? And just how much do you know about Mario anyway?"

Maya hadn't said anything before, but all India seemed to know about her new love was that he was attractive and widowed. She didn't know where he transferred from, and she never mentioned if he had any other family. Not once had she spoken of his parents, siblings, or any friends. To Maya, that was a bit strange.

"I have to get to know him, which is why we are going out Friday. And as far as my family is concerned, no one will ever know, Maya. I'm not trying to fall in love with the man; I just need a break from all the drama at home. It's not as serious as you're making it out to be," India answered nonchalantly, swerving around in her chair and placing her shapely legs on top of her desk.

Maya shook her head in disagreement but what was the point? India's mind was made up, and she'd just have to learn the hard way. After all, a lesson learned the hard way was the best lesson learned. Maya just hoped in the end that the affair wouldn't cost India more than her heart could afford to pay.

Looking up at the clock, Maya realized it was time for her to pick up her youngest son from daycare. "Just think about what I said, India. Having an affair is not the answer to your problems."

Before India could respond, Maya continued, "I've gotta go now. Love you."

"Love you, too," India said before placing the phone back on her desk. It would take some time, but Maya would come around. If not, they'd again agree to disagree. It wasn't the first time and wouldn't be the last.

Just as Maya reached the door, she felt a vaguely familiar knotting in her stomach. Stopping in her tracks as everything around her grew quiet, Maya stared absently out the window. As clear as day, she saw a woman and two men, one with cold, green eyes. She saw his face clearly, but the other two had their backs turned to her. The green-eyed man held a gun and within the blink of an eye, he fired it. The loud explosion rang in her ears and she stood frozen, staring out the window. Everything went black before she was able to see who had been shot.

Panting, Maya felt abnormally cold. She looked down at her arms and saw chill bumps amidst the fine hairs that stood at attention. The ticking of the clock was far louder than usual, and she could even hear the usually undetected humming of the air conditioning unit. Years had passed since she'd had a vision. She silently prayed that the *gift* had left her once and for all.

She rarely spoke of her psychic visions and debated as to whether or not she should try again to warn India. There was something very wrong with Mario Thomas, and India could be in grave danger.

Chapter 11

Friday night came, and I prepared for my encounter with Mario, against Maya's advice. I couldn't believe she had the nerve to claim she had a psychic vision. I'd known that girl since we were teenagers, and she'd never said shit about having no damn visions. If she had that power, she should have warned me about Trey's father, that no-good, two timing bastard! The fact that he would leave me pregnant and never be a part of our son's life would have been some much needed information.

I didn't believe that girl was psychic for a minute. If anything she was crazy as hell. I loved my friend dearly, but the whole *goody two shoe thing* had gotten old. Besides, I didn't have her perfect family. It must have been nice to be happily married to the man you shared three kids with. No baby mama drama and no meddling sisters interfering in your marriage. Maya had the good life and didn't have a clue how hard it was for me, trying to raise another woman's child and having to fight tooth and nail for any respect in my own damn home.

With Trey settled at my mother's for the weekend and Ariel at her grandmother's house, I rushed home. I wanted to be out of the house before Antoine got in from work. I'd fed him some lie about a cosmetic party with Maya. Every now and then I did make an appearance at her little bougie parties. But not tonight; tonight was finally all about me.

After a quick shower, I oiled my body, styled my long wrap, and slipped into my red gown. It was a short little number that fell about mid-thigh exposing my curvy hips and shapely legs. I slipped into matching red shoes, sat at my vanity, and applied my makeup. The salsa red lipstick was smoking. I blew myself a kiss before grabbing my keys and practically running to my car.

The Plaza was located on the outskirts of town. For the most part only the elite citizens of Crisp and surrounding counties dined there. The chance of me running into anyone Antoine and I knew was slim. But if by chance I did run into someone I knew, I could always introduce Mario as my boss, leaving the impression that our dinner was strictly business.

I pulled into the parking lot, in search of Mario's silver Lexus. I smiled widely when I read his personalized tag, *MTHNIC*, Mario Thomas Head Nigga In Charge. I parked my baby blue BMW right next to his beautiful car, took one final look in my compact and headed for the entrance. My heart skipped a beat when I entered the lobby informing the hostess that I was with the Thomas party of two.

Never in my life had I ever contemplated having an affair, but there I was following some young girl who didn't know she was leading Daniel into the lion's den.

Chapter 12

Beautiful did little to describe the beautiful creature who sashayed toward him. Mario almost stopped breathing when he looked up and saw her, following the waitress to his table. She was really there, in the flesh.

He rose from the table and awaited her arrival. He then pulled her chair out and stood back, allowing her to take a seat, before pushing the chair toward the table.

"Thank you," she spoke through those full red lips.

"No. Thank you for wearing that dress. May I say that you look gorgeous?" His eyes combed her body, a smile of approval adorning his handsome face, causing her to blush like a school girl.

"Yes, you may. Thank you." She giggled. He always made her feel so special. Those were feelings she missed being that Antoine and she were always busy with work and dealing with the kids. Rarely did he say kind words that made her feel as special as a woman should feel. But Mario, he always knew just what to say to make even her second set of lips form a smile.

He'd already ordered wine and after filling her empty flute, he suggested a toast. She raised her glass to his.

"To new beginnings," he said, giving her a seductive wink.

"To new beginnings," she repeated.

Half way through their meal, she thought back to some of her conversation with Maya, realizing she hadn't asked him anything about himself, nor had he offered. Just to have something to report back to Maya, she asked, "So where are you from?"

"I was born and raised in a small town in Louisiana," he said with a blank expression, offering no further details.

"Oh, and what about your family? Do they still live there?" India pressed for more about her mystery man.

Feeling uncomfortable, Mario laid his fork down on the table. He didn't like being interrogated, and he certainly didn't like to talk about his family. Damn if she wasn't acting like the damn shrink he'd seen a few months earlier, trying to get in his head. Well, she wasn't getting there. He'd allow her into his heart yes, but his head, never.

"We lost contact over the years. I learned years ago that I was adopted and my family and I haven't been close since. I felt it best to just sever all ties and move on," he lied. It was the same lie he'd told Sharon and countless doctors, including Dr. Martin, his most recent shrink. He'd almost broken him, but Mario was too smart for that. He got a transfer and left town, refusing to ever return to Dr. Martin's office for another *cry your eyes out* session.

"I'm sorry to hear that," she offered, before taking a sip of her wine.

For a few moments, his mind drifted back in time to his childhood on the bayou. Thoughts of his mother, father, and little brother, Johnny danced through his mind. Hit suddenly with a strong dose of nostalgia, he felt his eyes water at the many memories that flashed before him. Mario quickly changed the subject.

"So, now that you've drilled me, it's my turn," he teased. "Tell me about your family. Are you from this quiet town?"

"Yep, I was born and raised here in Cordele. My mother raised me and my brother after our father decided to come out of the closet and live a happy, gay life with his lover. As it turns out he loved his best friend more than he loved his young wife. Hell, he loved him more than he loved any of us apparently," her voice trailed off. He offered to refill her wine glass and she graciously accepted. "We never hear from him. Last I heard he and his lover were living in San Francisco."

"That must have been tough. I mean, losing your father to another man, wow," he said. Mario didn't know the man from Adam, but seeing the pain in India's eyes, he wanted to kill him. Men like him didn't deserve to live happily ever after having caused pain so great.

India shrugged her bare shoulders and mustered up a smile. "It's been years. No sense in crying over spilled milk. Besides, we have the best mother in the whole world, and she was blessed to find love again. Daddy Jordan was a wonderful husband and a damn good father to Ric and me."

"Was?" Mario questioned, gently placing his wine glass down on the table. He reached out and covered her hand with his own. She was shaking.

"He was killed about five years ago, a drunk driver. He died in Momma's arms," India managed to say as the tears threatened to spill over.

They sat in silence for a few moments, him gently stroking her trembling hands. Neither aware of the young waitress who watched them from the kitchen. She knew India and couldn't believe that she had the nerve to be there with another man.

"Listen, I don't want you to think the wrong thing about me," Mario said, "but I reserved a room for us upstairs. If I'm being too forward, just let me know. I just want some private time alone with you, if that's okay." He stared deeply into her eyes. She was so very beautiful, flawless. He loved her honey-dipped skin and her hazel eyes. Her full lips mesmerized him, and she was the perfect size and height, 5'5, not a pound more than 150.

She answered him with a warm smile, squeezing his hand and nodding affirmatively. Mario led the way to the elevator that would take them to their own personal heaven on the third floor.

Chapter 13

Mario made the first move. His full lips covered mine and I sucked the sweet wine residue from them. My body tingled immensely as my nipples hardened. Our kisses grew deeper and more passionate. His hands caressed my cheeks and my fingers stroked his soft curls. Just as I had imagined, his hair felt like silk.

Clothes were tossed to the side. Mario nestled his head between the parting of my thighs and devoured me like I was Sunday dinner at Big Momma's house. He licked, sucked, and nibbled my clit. His lips wrapped around mine as his tongue pierced through my heated opening. I almost lost my damn mind. I started speaking in a language even I myself didn't understand. His oral skills caused an earth shattering orgasm in a matter of a few moments. He was as good as he looked. Already he had me weak in my knees.

I returned the favor by taking him into my mouth inch by inch. His member wasn't as large as I had hoped, but I could work with it. I licked the head as I stroked the shaft. I then took the entire seven inches into my mouth. I swallowed his head and tickled it with my tonsils. That sent him into an explosive orgasm. The thick cum oozed down my throat and I savored the bittersweet taste of his release.

Reaching into my purse, I grabbed a condom. With my teeth, I tore into the wrapper and placed the latex barrier over his stiff erection. I straddled him, guided him into my burning furnace, and rode him like a jockey. He pulled my body forward and took both my nipples into the warmth of his mouth. Like a bolt of electricity, the pleasure shot through me and into my burning loins. He sucked until my nipples ached and I screamed out in pain. It was a good pain, a pain my body welcomed.

I gyrated my hips in a circular motion, left to right and then right to left. Mario grinded into me, pushing his throbbing flesh deeper into my wet abyss. He grabbed my ass and spread my cheeks apart. I gasped as he used a finger to penetrate my anus. This was more than I had imagined and I was enjoying every minute.

My lips covered his. One of his wide hands cupped and caressed both of my full breasts. My hands cradled his face. His other hand squeezed my ass as a single digit moved around my anus. My walls squeezed him tightly. Our eyes locked and within seconds my walls were contracting and his member was throbbing. I could feel his release and his facial expression told me he felt mine as my walls squeezed him tighter and tighter beyond my control.

"I've imagined this moment since the first time I laid eyes on you," he confessed. "I knew you would be good, but I didn't think it was possible for you to be this good!"

Having exceeded my own expectations, I blushed at his compliment. He was only the second man I'd had oral sex with. Hell, he was the third man I'd had intercourse with. But, he brought out something in me that every lady tries to keep hidden. He brought out the whore in me, that selfless side of me that housed no sexual inhibitions. With him, I was happy, even proud to be a whore.

"I aim to please." I bit my bottom lip seductively. "You were pretty damn good yourself. You know for an older brother."

"Thirty-seven is old now?" He pretended to be insulted, but I knew he wasn't. He had a wonderful sense of humor. "I guess I'll just kill myself when I turn forty. That's if you don't give me a heart attack first."

"I'll be gentle," I promised as I planted a wet kiss on his sexy lips.

We spent the rest of the evening soaking in the Jacuzzi, sipping on wine, and just getting to know each other. Well, at least me telling him more about my childhood. It felt good to just sit back and relax—no fussing and fighting, just pure relaxation. Mario massaged my tense shoulders and I nearly fell asleep in his arms.

Chapter 14

Every Friday night he confirmed what he knew to be true the first time he laid eyes on India. She did taste like Sharon, sweet as the morning dew, and her scent was intoxicating, rendering him a drunken fool in love.

With the close of each Friday night, he found it harder and harder to tear himself away from her embrace, not wanting to let her go back to that façade of a life that she put up with day in and day out. She needed him, and he wanted her more than words could ever explain.

She was his—his Sharon. So many times he'd almost screamed out her name in the heated throws of their passionate love making. Sharon. She had to be her. She sucked him with the same vigor. Her kitty purred to him, taking all of him inside of its heated abyss, fitting perfectly around his shaft like a glove. She even rocked him to the same beat of Sharon's drum.

The first time he laid eyes on her, he knew it was her. Not much had changed. She had the same beautiful eyes, pearly white teeth, and the classiest walk. Her voice was soft, and her scent easily aroused him. India Joiner was his late wife, she had to be. If she wasn't Sharon that meant that Dr. Martin was right; he was losing his mind, and that couldn't be.

Chapter 15

"I can't believe you're still seeing him." Maya and India were having lunch at their favorite Italian bar and grill.

Maya rolled her eyes and sighed in disgust before continuing. "I keep warning you about this man, but still you rush to The Plaza every Friday. When are you going to take heed and let it go, India?"

Maya could tell by the nonchalant shrug of her friend's shoulders that she didn't take her visions seriously, but Maya knew better. Visions she had as a child often matured into reality, quite accurately. She wished she hadn't seen the vision of her grandparents trapped in a fire at their cottage home because within months they both succumbed to fiery deaths, burned beyond recognition. For a long time she blamed herself for being too timid to tell her parents about the vision, too scared they'd think she was crazy.

India still didn't know much about Mario being that he wouldn't open up and talk about his past. Even though India didn't think much of it, Maya knew that was a fire burning, red flag. He was hiding something behind those green eyes but her girl was so caught up in his loving that she chose to turn a blind eye to the warning signs. Maya knew as soon as India fed her that bullshit about him being adopted and estranged from his family that something stank like sour milk in a hot refrigerator in the middle of July.

India had grown quiet, not wanting to argue about Mario anymore. She knew what she needed to know about him. He, unlike Antoine, made her happy instead of angry and tense all the time. With him she could smile and enjoy life, even if it was only one day out of the week. For her it was the best day out of the week, and the past four weeks with him had been better than the last year of her marriage.

As if she was able to read her friend's thoughts, Maya asked, "What about home? How are things with your family?"

India opened her mouth to answer but realized she didn't know what to say. Instead of speaking, she just stared blankly at her friend. She was so caught up in Mario that she paid very little attention to Antoine and the kids. She couldn't remember her last fight with Ariel or Antoine. Sadly, she didn't even know what was going on with Trey, her own child. At home all she did was fantasize about Mario, detaching herself from everyone around her.

"I honestly don't know," she finally mumbled, laying her fork down on the napkin next to her plate. She didn't have enough appetite to finish her grilled chicken salad as she realized just how much the affair was changing her. Normally she was very attentive to her family, especially her son. She always knew what was going on with him. Suddenly, she felt like less than a mother, unable to remember the last time she helped him with homework or even asked him about school. Consumed with guilt, her heart ached and tears raced, uncontrollably, down her face.

Tears welled into Maya's own eyes as she watched her friend slowly drift back to planet Earth. She reached her hand across the table, gently placing it over India's. She spoke softly, her voice laced with genuine love and concern. "You have to end this, India. If Antoine finds out, things are going to get bad, and I don't want to see you in any more pain than you're in right now, hon."

India nodded her head in agreement, knowing that she couldn't continue to hide behind the affair with Mario. She had to face her family problems head on. Either she and Antoine could work things out, or if it came to it, they'd have to part ways. Maybe they could go to family counseling, him, her, and the kids. If it would save their marriage, she was willing to give it a try.

"I'm going to meet Mario Friday and end things quietly over dinner," India announced while using a napkin to dry her tears.

Maya began to smile but no sooner than she did, she felt that familiar feeling creeping up on her. She stared absently out the restaurant's bay window. Again she was deaf to the sounds around her. India saw all the color rush from Maya's face and wondered just what the hell was going on.

"Maya, are you okay? Maya?" India yelled repeatedly.

Again, Maya saw the vision, a woman and two men, one with cold, green eyes. She saw all their faces clearly now, Mario, India, and Antoine. Mario had a sinister grin on his face, and he held a gun in his hand. The next thing Maya saw was India's mouth open wide in a gut-wrenching scream, and there was blood, lots of blood. A woman then appeared out of thin air, grieving. The others didn't seem to notice her. She was tall, her physique curvaceous. Her light skin was flawless; her silky, black hair wrapped in a stylish bob. The woman looked up, eyes filled with tears. Maya gasped. Her eyes, they were so familiar, hazel with specks of green. It was her! Maya was staring face to face at her own image.

"Oh my God," she screamed, not knowing what to make of her vision's creepy ending. She was breathing rapidly and could hear the clink of every dish in the restaurant. Everything was so loud, and she was so cold. She wrapped her arms around her shoulders.

"Maya, what is it? What's wrong?" India was in tears again, having no idea what was going on with Maya. *Had she had a seizure? Was she having some kind of stroke or heart attack? Why did she feel like a block of ice?*

"You can't meet him, India. Some how Antoine is going to show up and I think Mario is going to shoot him," she warned. She didn't mention the part of the vision where she was grieving. Maya wasn't quite sure how that tied in to everything else. Was she grieving the loss of her friend? Or was she getting ready to face some of her own demons that would leave her in despair?

Chapter 16

Jay had been toying with the idea of telling his best friend, Antoine about his wife for weeks. He was left shocked after a phone call from his cousin, Kia, informing him that she'd been seeing India dining at The Plaza with some older dude. At first he thought maybe it was just an innocent business dinner, but then Kia went on to tell him how the two always ended up upstairs in one of the expensive suites. After his own investigation, Jay determined that the man was Mario Thomas, India's new boss at Cordelia Bank.

He wanted to tell Antoine, but not before he was sure it was true. Now that he knew, without doubt, that his best friend's wife was in fact creeping, he had to tell him. The news was going to devastate Antoine though, being that he loved India more than a fly loved shit. Jay admired their relationship, having yet to find that special love of his own. The last thing he wanted was to believe that India would cheat on Antoine but the truth was just that, the truth.

The two men were on their way home after a long day at the Pepsi plant. Antoine was on the passenger side of Jay's gold Expedition. They took turns driving and this was Jay's week.

Before speaking, Jay cleared his throat and turned the radio's volume down.

"What up with that, man?" Antoine asked when Jay turned the volume down on Rick Ross's latest jam. The bass from the speakers somehow soothed and relaxed him; whereas, most people complained about the deafening effects of the constant *BOOM, BOOM!*

"I need to holla at you 'bout something real serious, bro," Jay said, pulling into the parking lot of a local pool room. They normally went straight home after work during the week, but Jay knew Antoine would need some time to cool off after hearing his news. He decided to treat him to a burger, a cold beer, and a few games of pool.

"Speak, black man," Antoine told his friend once they were seated, their food orders taken.

"This ain't the kind of thing I wanna have to tell my boy, but I can't keep this shit from you either," Jay said, taking a long gulp of his Budweiser.

Antoine didn't like the tone in Jay's voice, it was too serious. Whatever Jay had to tell him, he needed to hurry up and spit it out so they could deal with it. Antoine wasn't one for beating around nobody's bush.

Under Antoine's intense stare, Jay continued, "My cousin Kia works out at that fancy resort, The Plaza, and she said India's been coming in there with a dude every Friday."

For a few seconds, neither man blinked an eye as they sat staring across the table at each other. Antoine was deaf to the sounds surrounding him, the clashing of the pool balls, the caching of the slot machines, the idle chatter and laughter from the other patrons. To others it would appear that he was staring at his friend's mocha-chocolate face, but Antoine was looking beyond Jay. He was racking his brain, trying to find reasons why Jay's news couldn't be true.

"Ant, you okay, bro?" Jay asked as his friend sat speechless and expressionless. Antoine's light eyes suddenly looked dark and cold as if they bore no soul behind them.

Finally, he spoke, his voice monotone. "Who is he? Who's the dude?" he asked his best friend before calmly picking up his bottle of Heineken and taking a long swig.

Stunned at his friend's calmness, Jay answered, "Mario Thomas, her boss."

All Antoine could do was nod as he continued to finish off his beer. He didn't even taste it going down, just knew it was gone after a few minutes. He ordered another one when the young waitress returned with their burgers and fries. She wasn't an attractive woman but in that moment, he wanted to fuck her just to get back at his wife, so he flirted with her.

"What's your name, Sexy?" he asked, licking his lips like LL Cool J.

The young woman giggled before saying, "Tyra." The man speaking to her looked like a dark skinned version of Allen Iverson, even sexier in chocolate. She could see herself looking down into his handsome face while riding him into the wee hours of the night.

"Tyra, huh? You got a man, Tyra?" he asked, pretending not to see the confused and shocked expression on Jay's face.

The pimply faced girl shook her head no and he continued in player mode. "Want one? Think you can handle a real man like me?"

Jay had heard enough. "Can we get the check, please?" he asked the girl before she could answer. He knew the chick was ready to give up more than her phone number. She didn't know Antoine from Adam, but already she was ready to give up the panties and do whatever. Once she was out of hearing range, he said to Antoine, "What the fuck was that about? That broad couldn't be a day over twenty."

"What? Twenty is legal," Antoine defended, taking down his second beer in one swig. He shrugged his shoulders nonchalantly and smiled. "You think my wife is the only one who can play the field?"

Jay sighed deeply. He should've known Antoine would try to mask his pain but the last thing he needed was to get caught up in an affair of his own. After watching his own brother succumb to AIDS, Jay was tired of the single player's life. He envied the life Antoine and India shared. Even though she'd crossed the line, putting them both at risk of HIV and other STD's, Jay didn't want Antoine to do the same, doubling their risk.

"I know you don't wanna hear this right now, but crawling up in somebody else's ass ain't the answer to your marital problems. You don't know shit about Tyra, and the last thing you need to do is fuck her and find out some shit you don't want to know later on. If she's this eager to get with you, you best believe her ass has been around." Jay finished off his own beer. "What you need to do is talk things out with your wife and decide if your marriage is worth saving."

"She told me she was at Mary Kay parties with Maya," Antoine said just above a whisper. "Every Friday, she told me she was out with Maya and I didn't question her, man. I never had no reason to believe my wife would cheat on me. We have problems, mainly dealing with Ariel and Rachel, but I didn't think it would come to this, some other dude running up in my woman. How do I recover from that, Jay? How can I go home and face her, knowing that she's been giving my pussy to some punk ass mo'fucka?"

In that moment, Antoine wanted to kill them both, the woman he loved and the man who disrespected him. He was shocked that Maya knew about the affair, but he knew he couldn't blame her. She didn't make India go out and fuck that mo'fucka. Knowing her she tried to talk India out of it, just like Jay talked him out of dragging Tyra into their drama.

"You gotta talk to her, man. There's no way around that. But if you need somewhere to crash for awhile, you know you can always stay at my place," Jay offered.

"I just may have to take you up on that," he told Jay. He wasn't sure if he could stay in the house with India without hurting her. He was convinced he'd be haunted by images of her with another man every time he looked at her. A sharp pain shot through his chest. Maybe it was his own fault that she'd had an affair. Maybe he should have done more to resolve matters between she and Ariel. But what was he to do, choose his wife over his daughter?

Chapter 17

Looking at the clock, I realized Antoine was more than an hour late. It was after eight o'clock and the kids and I finished our dinner before I sent them upstairs to take their baths. I realized that Ariel was more cooperative than usual, and I couldn't help but to wonder when her attitude changed for the better. She wasn't back to the little girl I had grown to love in the beginning, but she wasn't exactly the evil little princess I'd deemed her to be either. We made it through homework and dinner without any harsh words. She even thanked me for helping her with the math assignment she was having trouble with.

I felt like a stranger in my own house, not knowing what kind of dinners we'd had over the past few weeks. My mind was so focused on my Fridays with Mario that I mechanically lived a robotic existence during the week. I was sure I'd been cooking and cleaning, but I couldn't recall any details, yet I knew every position I'd lain in with Mario. I could describe his masculine smell, his taste, the feel of his hair, and the way he made me feel but nothing outside of our paradise held my attention. I'd really lost my fucking mind over that man.

I thought about calling him up and ending things over the phone, giving more thought to Maya's warning, but just as I reached for my cell phone, I heard Antoine enter through the carport door.

"What's up?" I asked looking from him to the kitchen clock on the wall.

"Jay and I stopped for a couple beers and burgers," he answered, no emotion reflected in his voice.

"On a Wednesday?" That wasn't like him. Something about the way he was acting was out of character, and I wanted to know what was going on. "Is everything okay, Ant?" I asked.

I was standing at our kitchen counter, hand washing pots and pans. He stood on the other side of the counter facing me. Before speaking, he stared deeply into my eyes, sending chills up my spine. "Is everything okay, *wifey?*"

Nervously, I chuckled. "Everything's fine on this end, *hubby.* Your plate is in the microwave if you want it. I cooked pork chops, lima beans, and rice." I busied myself with the dishes trying to ignore his glare.

"I know, India," he finally said.

"Know what?" I asked, my eyes filling with tears. How could he know? How in the fuck could he find out now when I was getting ready to end the shit? He couldn't know. He just couldn't know! Maybe I was overreacting and he was talking about something else. Maybe he knew about the secret savings account I had on the side. Every woman had a nest egg though; it was no big deal.

"Don't play games with me, India. I'm trying real hard not to lose my cool, so don't fucking lie to me," he yelled, causing me to drop the glass pan I held in my hands. It crashed to the floor, breaking in a loud thump. "I know you fucking your boss, and you been lying to me every Friday to meet him at The Plaza. So, don't fucking stand here now and lie to my face."

I bent down to pick up the broken pieces of the dish, but he yelled at me again. "Leave it. Look at me and tell me the truth. You fucking him?" he demanded to know. A storm was raging within my husband. His voice boomed like loud clashes of thunder and in his eyes I saw flashes of sharp lightning.

Scared, I didn't know what to say. I opened my mouth to speak and that's when I heard my son's voice. "Mommy, you okay?" I turned to the staircase to see he and Ariel standing there, their tear-filled eyes stretched wide open. They'd never witnessed anything this bad between Antoine and me. We argued but never like this.

"I'm okay, baby," I managed to say between sobs. "You and Ariel go upstairs and go to bed. I'll be up in a few minutes."

For a minute, he didn't move, my nine-year-old boy stood tall like a man wanting to protect his mother, regardless of the situation. He stared Antoine down, silently but firmly warning him not to harm the woman who carried him, birthed him, and loved him beyond words. Again, I told him, "I'll be up in a few minutes. Everything's okay, Trey." I admired my son's display of bravado, but it wasn't his fight; it was mine and mine alone.

Once I was sure the kids were in their rooms, I mustered up the courage to face Antoine. "I love you so much, and I am so sorry—"

"Sorry, huh?" He laughed sarcastically. "Is that your way of telling me that it's true?"

"It's true," I admitted. "It's true and I'm sorry for lying to you, baby. I'm going to end things, I promise. I don't love him, I love you, Antoine," I cried.

I moved toward him, but he held his hand out, stopping me in my tracks. Just as he wouldn't let me pick up the broken glass, he wouldn't let me attempt to fix our broken marriage.

"I'm going upstairs to pack my shit," he said, backing away from me, his face twisted in pure disgust. "I'm going to stay with Jay because right now, I can't stand to look at you. Just the sight of you makes me sick to my fucking stomach. If I stay here, I can't be responsible for what I may do to you, India."

As he walked hurriedly up the stairs, I ran behind him, begging and pleading, trying to explain my actions. Unaffected by my deafening cries, Antoine continued his plight up the stairs. Once inside our bedroom, he opened the closet door and threw luggage on our bed before snatching several work uniforms from their hangers. He packed his bags, refusing to look at me, speak to me, or even acknowledge my presence. I fell down to my knees, my stomach in knots. "Antoine, please! Please don't leave. Please, baby. I'm so sorry." I cried hysterically.

"I'm sorry, too, India. I'm sorry for wasting six years of my life with you," he snarled. I could hear the pain in his voice; his eyes glistened with tears. The storm raged; booming thunder and sharp lightning, as sheets of tears threatened to rain from his eyes.

Suitcase filled with toiletries, most of his casual belongings, and work clothes, he stormed downstairs, out the carport door, and out of my life. When I heard the engine of his Caprice come to life, I died a thousand deaths on our bedroom floor, heartbroken with no one to blame but me.

Chapter 18

Maya held the phone to her right ear, listening intently as India poured out the remains of her shattered heart. Antoine knew about the affair and he'd packed his clothes and left with no word as to if or when he would return. Of course India was devastated, and Maya felt her best friend's pain.

"How did he find out?" she asked. She knew she hadn't told him and India wasn't one to put her business out there. Besides each other, the two of them didn't have many acquaintances, especially anyone they considered close friends. Their only other trusted friend was Candi, who lived in Chicago, and not even she knew of the affair. India was too embarrassed to tell her and Maya knew it wasn't her place.

"I don't know, girl. He came home an hour later than normal, but I don't know if that has anything to do with him knowing. I was so shocked when he questioned me about it that I didn't even bother asking how he knew. I think that would have only made matters worse." India sobbed.

Having called in sick from work, she was at home lying in bed. She didn't want to face Mario or the world in general after losing the love of her life. After driving the kids to school, she returned home and called Maya, ignoring the calls and text messages on her cell phone from Mario.

"I can imagine it would have," Maya agreed. "But, do you think he just needs time to cool off? I mean, he did leave Ariel there after all and you'd think if he was leaving you for good he would have taken his daughter with him."

India had given that some thought. She too was shocked when both kids came in to comfort her after Antoine stormed out. She was lying face down on the bedroom floor when she felt small hands rubbing her back. She looked up to see both Trey and Ariel, tears streaming down their faces. Few words were spoken, but for the first time in a long time, India felt a loving connection with her stepdaughter. Both kids slept next to her in the king size bed she'd grown accustomed to sharing with her husband.

"Maybe. I hope that's all. Then again, maybe he just needs time to get a place for the two of them. I don't know, Maya. I just know that I fucked up big time."

Maya couldn't disagree with that, but she wasn't about to throw an *I told you so* in India's face. That's the last thing she needed to hear. Instead of rubbing her face in it, Maya said, "How about I go and get us some breakfast, and then we can sit around all day watching talk shows and combing each other's hair." She laughed lightly, hoping to lighten the mood.

"Are you sure? I don't want to take you out of your daily routine," India responded, appreciative for the offer because she didn't want to be alone either. Every inch of the house held countless memories of her years with Antoine, and with him gone, she felt as if she was dying second by second. Even with the sun shining brightly, India felt surrounded by darkness.

"I'll be there in about an hour," Maya said. They both said their goodbyes and hung up. As she dressed, Maya debated talking to India about her own past, sharing with her the one thing that not even her first love, or even her own husband knew about her. She'd done well to bury her past but now the visions were bringing it all back. She could run from it, but obviously she couldn't hide, not from herself. The past was a part of her and no matter how far she ran, it would always catch her; the past would always be a part of her.

She still wasn't sure just what the end of her vision meant, had no clue as to why she could vividly see herself dressed in all black, crying, obviously in mourning. Surely her secret wouldn't lead to death. Tony would be angry, may even walk out on her, but he certainly wouldn't hurt himself or anyone else.

She suddenly remembered that Tony was still insecure about her past love for Ric. Would the secret push his insecurities over the edge, building up to an old western showdown between Ric and him, and if so, who would be left standing?

Her long bob swung freely as she shook her head from side to side laughing to herself. "I'm just being silly," she said, grabbing her keys as she walked toward the front door. But even in her moment of silliness, she decided it best not to tell India or anyone else about her little secret. She had to figure out the vision before she risked losing someone she loved, Ric or Tony. She lost Ric to his wife Sonya years ago, but she'd be damned if she lost him or Tony for eternity.

Chapter 19

Mario slammed his fist on the mahogany desk in front of him. India wasn't in her office today and she'd yet to return any of his calls or text messages. He was out of his mind worrying about her. Now that they were so close to being together for eternity, he feared that she may be backing away from him. He couldn't let that happen, not now that he almost had his beloved back in his arms.

Her actions were interfering with his plans. The time had come for him to get rid of that *husband* of hers and for the two of them to leave Cordele once and for all. Getting her away from the little town was the only way she would remember their past together. As long as she was surrounded by people who knew her as India, she'd never completely be his Sharon.

As if he didn't have enough problems to deal with, he received a letter from that quack Dr. Martin as well, telling him all the reasons he needed to continue with his meds and come to his office for therapy sessions. He balled the paper up and threw it into the trash receptacle.

He wasn't crazy. If anything Dr. Martin was the one who needed help. The man didn't know how to take no for a fucking answer. He'd told him over and over that he didn't need his help. After all, he wasn't delusional, he saw things very clearly. And he wasn't repressing any memories from the past; he simply chose not to share his history with Dr. Martin or anyone else. He didn't need anybody judging him never having known anything about his life in Louisiana.

The doctor claimed he was afraid that Mario might harm himself or someone else if he didn't take his medication and seek help soon. He had a good mind to drive thirty miles south to Tifton and choke the life out of that Dr. Martin. To think, he almost—almost told that shrink everything about his past. Good thing he stopped himself before it was too late. He knew there was such a thing as patient-doctor confidentiality, but he didn't trust Dr. Martin to keep his mouth closed had he told him the real deal about his severed ties back in Louisiana. The man would have surely gone screaming to the authorities.

Hearing his cell phone chime, Mario reached inside his coat pocket to retrieve it. He had one new message. He flipped his phone open and smiled when he saw who the message was from.

Meet me in my office in the morning, 9 sharp. We need to talk.

"It won't be long now, my love," he said aloud.

Chapter 20

"Are you sure this is what you want to do?" Maya asked India after she'd sent the text message to Mario. "I mean it's better than going ahead and meeting him at The Plaza, but if you need me, I'm there. I don't trust you alone with this guy."

India closed her phone and laid it back down on the nightstand next to her bed. She wasn't afraid of being alone with Mario, especially not in her office. She knew he was too much of a professional to create a scene. She trusted that he would accept the end of their affair and move on to the next woman. After all that is what men were famous for doing and with his pretty boy features, he'd have no problem moving on. Half the women at the bank were throwing themselves at him, fantasizing about being the woman he stared at lovingly through those mesmerizing green eyes.

"I'll be fine," she assured Maya. "Besides, I got mace."

Both women laughed for a moment. They'd spent the entire morning watching episodes of Maury Povich, AKA *you are not the father*. It cracked the both of them up to see the women sitting up there screaming and crying that they were over one hundred percent sure that the men were the fathers of their babies, only to have Maury read negative DNA test results. Why those women went up there making fools of themselves, neither Maya nor India knew. They just knew they rolled their eyes in disgust each time the ladies left the stage, running and screaming before falling out on a nearby couch, chair, or the ever convenient floor.

"So, you haven't heard from Antoine at all, I guess?" Maya asked. They were now downstairs in the kitchen eating finger sandwiches and white grapes. India wasn't up to cooking or going out for lunch. She was, however, up for finishing off a bottle of white wine she had chilling in the refrigerator. She wasn't an alcoholic, but the wine sure helped to calm her nerves.

"Not once. I thought about calling him, but I'm sure he's at work. Besides, I'm not sure my heart can take what he may have to say to me right about now. As hard as it is, I'm trying to give him space and time to cool off." India sipped slowly from the wine glass.

Maya finished chewing her last bite of sandwich and washed it down with a sip of wine before replying. "I'm sure he'll call soon. And you're right, let him cool off because what he may say in anger now may not be what he truly means."

The two finished their snacks and returned upstairs for more talk show TV. India's cell phone chimed from the nightstand and she reached over to look at the Caller ID. She'd been ignoring the persistent calls from Mario. If it was him again, she was sending his ass straight to voicemail—again.

"It's him," she said to Maya before answering. "Hello?"

"Hey," was all he said initially.

"Hey." She couldn't think of much to say either. She'd been dying for him to call, but now that he was on the phone she was two seconds from peeing all over herself. To say she had butterflies was an understatement. She felt as if she had bricks in her stomach.

"I know you're probably wondering why I left Ariel."

"Well, it's not a problem. She can stay as long as–"

He cut her off before she could finish. "I don't know what's going to happen between us, India. I just know I don't want to confuse Ariel by dragging her out of our home and into another one. If I decide that it's over for us, I'll find a place for the two of us."

Maya gathered from India's end of the conversation that the *him* on the other end was Antoine. She quietly excused herself to the restroom to relieve her bladder and offer them some privacy.

"I, uh, well, that's fine with me," she agreed. Prior to his call she knew everything she wanted to say to him, but now that he was on the phone, her mind drew blank.

Again, silence rang loudly. He didn't know what else to say and she was so afraid of saying the wrong thing, pushing him even farther away than he already was.

"Antoine, I'm sorry," she blurted out, ending the deafening silence. "I miss you so much and I," tears rendered her unable to complete her sentence.

"I know," he said, looking at his watch. "Listen, I gotta get back to work, lunch is over. Maybe we can sit down and talk in a day or two."

"Maybe tomorrow night?" She was ready to see him and resolve things as quickly as possible. Being in that house, in their bedroom, in their bed without him, it just wasn't natural.

"Maybe. I'll give you a call tomorrow and we'll see. Bye, India."

That said he hung up before she could even say *good-bye* to him. Flipping her phone closed, she held it close to her heart. At least there was hope of salvaging their marriage.

"You okay?"

India looked up, almost surprised to see Maya standing next to her. She'd allowed herself to forget that her best friend was even there. She didn't hear her get up or come back into the bedroom.

India nodded her head affirmatively. "It was Antoine. He's going to call me tomorrow and let me know if we can sit down and talk. Until he decides about us, Ariel's going to stay here with Trey and me."

Knowing how strained the relationship was between India and Ariel, Maya asked the obvious. "Are you okay with that? Do you think Ariel's going to be okay with it?"

India smiled, sharing the story of the night before with Maya. Ariel surprised the both of them by being so affectionate and empathetic toward her stepmother.

"Wow," was all Maya could utter.

"This morning before school, I told them that Antoine and I were having a disagreement and that he was going to stay with Jay for a few days. They both asked if he'd be coming back, and I could only tell them that I was praying so. Ariel said she'd be praying for that, too, because she loved having a home with a mommy and daddy," India finished with a smile, still in utter disbelief. After all the fighting and animosity, she was shocked to learn that Ariel truly did love her.

"Who woulda thunk it?" Maya laughed. In a more serious tone she continued. "Children are so complex though. One minute they hate you, the next minute they love you more than chocolate fudge. It doesn't matter if they're your birth children or your stepchildren. In Ariel's case she's been through a lot.

"There's no telling what kind of poison Rachel fed that child's mind. She has to be confused which is why she acts out toward you, the stepmother, and when you react in a negative way, she believes the lies her mother has told her, that you don't care about her. I can't imagine what it's been like for either of you."

India absorbed her friend's words, allowing them to marinate on her brain. The words Maya spoke made perfect sense. She could only wish she'd taken a step outside the situation to look at it from every perspective before allowing things to get so out of control, before allowing herself to seek a stress reliever in the arms of another man.

"How is it that I'm so screwed up, and you're so freaking perfect?" India picked up a pillow and playfully hit Maya across the face with it.

"Perfect? Nah, I'm not perfect. Older and wiser, maybe, but perfect, not even close."

Again Maya toyed with the idea of confessing her past to India. Again she decided not to. India was dealing with enough already; she didn't need the weight of Maya's burdens upon her already slumping shoulders.

"Girl, please, you're only two years older than me, but you always have it together. You've got the perfect husband, a man who loves you beyond the description of any word in the English language. Not to mention those three handsome sons. And, oh, did I forget, me as a best friend?"

Both women fell into uncontrollable laughter and it felt great. In that moment, Maya didn't worry about facing her past, and India didn't ponder over what the future may hold. Together, they embraced the present and the happiness they felt in that moment.

Chapter 21

By the time nine o'clock rolled around, I was on my fourth cup of coffee, black, no cream, and two scoops of sugar. Dressed casually in black slacks and an off white shirt, I paced my office floor, nearly walking the heel off my black pumps, in anticipation of Mario's arrival. I was ready to put our affair behind me and hopefully salvage a future with my husband.

I looked down at my watch again; it was five minutes after nine. *Where the hell is he*? He was never late for our meetings at The Plaza. There wasn't one time that I got there and he wasn't already there, waiting, smiling, with wine already ordered. *Typical of a man to show up extra early for a booty call but not for a dismissal,* I thought angrily.

"Mrs. Joiner, Mr. Thomas is here to see you," Teresa's voice squealed over the intercom. It sounded like she was trying to sound extra sexy for Mario, as usual, but today it didn't matter. She could have him with my blessings.

I ran over to my desk and pressed the Intercom button to reply. "Send him in, Teresa, and hold my calls until this meeting is over." Before opening the door, I wiped my sweaty hands on the front of my pants.

"Good morning," he casually greeted, shaking my hand in front of Teresa.

"Good morning," I replied.

"Can I get you two anything, coffee, tea, anything at all?" Teresa offered, her eyes lingering on Mario. When we both declined, she quietly closed the door, leaving us to our *meeting.*

"I missed you yesterday. I do hope you're feeling okay." Mario walked toward me, his arms outstretched for an embrace.

"I'm fine," I answered, taking a step back toward my desk. "Please, have a seat."

He stood there for a minute, a puzzled look glued to his face. I took a seat and instructed him to sit across from me.

Taking note of the seriousness in my tone, he sat and asked, "Is there something wrong, Sharon? Is everything okay?"

"Sharon?" I sat forward, leaning across my desk, not sure I'd heard him correctly. "Did you just call me by your late wife's name?"

"Forgive me," he apologized. "Today would have been her birthday, and I'm just having a hard time dealing with that."

"I'm sorry. I know that must be painful, which makes what I have to say that much more difficult." I had no idea it was her birthday, but still I had to end the affair. There was no sense in dragging it on for yet another day.

A sad look crept into his green eyes, replacing the usual twinkle. His forehead wrinkled into a frown, his eyebrows raised into a question. "What's wrong? I hope it's nothing I've done to hurt or offend you."

If I sat there a minute longer, inhaling his masculinity, playing into his vunerability, I'd never end things. So the words shot out of my mouth like a bullet. "We're over, Mario. My husband somehow found out about us, and I told you from the very beginning that couldn't happen."

He stood from his chair, and in a flash he, in his gray Armani suit was down on his knees in front of me. "I didn't say a word, baby. How could he know?"

Feeling his hot breath on my thighs, I quickly rolled my chair away from him, stood and walked to the window. I heard him scramble back to his feet. I couldn't deny that I was still attracted to him, but my love for Antoine was stronger than my lust for Mario. I wouldn't give in to temptation, not this time.

"I don't know how he knows, but what matters is he knows," I answered matter-of-factly, folding my arms across my chest. With my back to Mario, I looked down at the waterfall in the park. Though I tried not to, I couldn't help but think back to the day we stood next to the same waterfall, planning our affair. If only I could take it all back, undo the damage that had been done to my marriage, and my heart.

"We can be more discreet," he whispered in my ear. The warmth of his breath against my ear was mesmerizing. "We can figure out a way to be together, but I can't lose you again, Sharon. I just won't."

Again, he called me by his dead wife's name. *What is his problem*? I turned to face him, almost afraid of what I saw when I looked at him. The look in his eyes was that of a man lonely to the point of obsession.

"I'm not Sharon, Mario," I declared. Confused by his behavior, my head shook, almost involuntarily, from side to side.

"Baby, we don't have to keep playing these games. Just let me take you away from this place and these people who won't let us live our lives in peace. You don't have to keep pretending to be someone else, Sharon." Again he fell to his knees, begging me to be someone I wasn't, someone I couldn't be, someone I didn't want to be—his dead wife.

"Mario, it's time for you to leave." I rushed over to the door. Maya had been right all along, there was something very wrong with him. No wonder he had nothing to say of his past; he was a nut case!

"Sharon, don't do this, please. Don't shut me out, baby. We were so close, so close to having our life together back."

My heart was pounding nearly out of my chest and I was on the verge of screaming for Teresa to call security when there was a knock at the door. As if awakened back to reality by the knock, Mario sprang to his feet, brushing imaginary dirt away from the knees of his expensive suit.

I quickly composed myself, taking a deep breath before opening my door. It was Teresa.

"I know you said to hold your calls, but it's your husband on line one. I figured you may want to take it," she said, not knowing just how accurate her assumption was.

"Yes, I do. Thanks, Teresa." Leaving the door open, I turned to Mario. "Mr. Thomas, thanks for taking the time out for this meeting. I hope you have a nice day."

"My pleasure," he said aloud. He then leaned in close to me and whispered. "See you tonight, my love."

Before I could protest he was already on the elevator, waving goodbye. I didn't know what was wrong with him, but I knew he needed some serious help. He could think he was going to see me at The Plaza, but by closing time even his crazy ass would realize it wasn't going down.

Running around to my desk, I answered the blinking line that my husband was holding on.

"Hello? Antoine?" I spoke into the receiver.

"I didn't mean to interrupt your meeting with *Mr.* Thomas," he said sarcastically.

"Antoine, it's not like that. I had to end things and that's it. You never have to worry about him or any other man again," I solemnly promised.

"And how can I be so sure of that, India? You and him work together. How do I know what's going on behind closed office doors when you're at work?"

So that's how it was going to be, no trust. I'd prove my loyalty to him at any cost.

"Antoine, I can always quit this job and find another one. I'll do whatever it takes to make things right between us."

He was quiet for a few moments before he spoke again. "I took today off, India. I'm at the house. I wanna pick the kids up from school and talk to them, and then we can talk when you get in."

My heart sank a bit, not sure what decision he had reached. His talking to the kids could mean that he was ready for a permanent move. Or maybe he was ready to come back home. Not knowing was killing me.

"I can leave work now, so we can talk. I can be there in five min–"

"Give me time to think, India. I'll be here when you get off, no rush," he said and hung up.

I could feel my heart oozing in my toes by that time. It felt like it had been stumped on. Not feeling up to doing any work, I reclined in my chair and called Maya. I had to fill her in on what was going on between Antoine and me, as well as let her know about that crazy ass Mario calling me by his deceased wife's name. I didn't know what was up with him, but if it walked like a duck and quacked like a duck, what else could it be? Mario was a lunatic!

Chapter 22

"Didn't I tell you that fool was crazy?" Maya said after listening to India recount her break up meeting with Mario.

"It was so weird though, hearing him call me by his dead wife's name. I mean at first he said it was a slip of the tongue, today being his wife's birthday and all. I let it go because I could understand him missing his wife. But then he said it again and again with a really disturbed look on his face. He was trying to convince me that I was Sharon. Can you believe that? He was determined to make me be a dead woman." Just thinking about the encounter brought chills to India's spine.

"Hell yeah I can believe it, and you better believe you need to stay far away from that fool," Maya said as she repositioned the phone between her shoulder and ear and continued folding laundry. "He may actually try to kidnap your ass or something. Hell, he's got me wondering if his wife peacefully died in his arms or if his crazy ass killed her."

"Well why don't you conjure up one of your psychic visions and tell me what really happened to Sharon Thomas?" India half-teased. She actually wouldn't mind if Maya could close her eyes and tell her everything there was to know about Mario. A part of her was truly afraid of what he could be capable of. She felt like an idiot for getting involved with him, knowing so little about him.

"Ha, I see you still got jokes but that's alright. I don't conjure up visions, they come when they come. And the next time I share one with you, your non-believing ass better take heed," Maya warned firmly.

With a roll of her eyes, India changed the subject. "Any-hoo. I am scared shitless about what may be waiting for me at home. Girl, what if I walk in the house and Antoine has all his shit packed. Or better yet, what if he has my shit packed since I'm the one who fucked up?"

"Positive thoughts," Maya encouraged her friend. "Be positive."

"Okay, I'm positive that I'm going to walk in and see my shit packed up by the front door." India laughed.

Maya bent down to pull more clothes from the dryer, but suddenly her stomach was in knots and everything was quiet. Again, as if she were in a trance, she stared absently, this time at the wall. The phone fell to the floor. Another vision showed the same scene that had been playing in her head. India, Antoine, and Mario—the blood, not one thing changed. Again the vision ended with her dressed in black, grieving. The vision was so real that she felt as though she could have reached out and touched herself.

"Maya! Maya, are you okay?"

Coming to, she finally heard India's voice booming from the receiver.

She picked up the phone and panting for breath, she answered her. "India, get out of there," she screamed.

"Maya, what are you talking about? What's wrong?"

"I just had the same vision, India. You and Antoine are still in danger. You've got to get out of that office and don't ever go back." Maya was in tears now, her heart was racing and she felt so cold.

"But, it's over, Maya. I'm not meeting Mario at The Plaza or anywhere else. Calm down, everything's going to be fine," India tried to reassure her.

Maya thought it was over, too, but according to her vision, it had yet to begin. "India, please, just–"

"Okay already, Maya. It's lunchtime. I'll bring lunch to your house. That way you can see that I'm fine. There's no need to panic." India grabbed her purse and prepared to leave the office.

"India, be careful. Please, just be careful," Maya said before hanging up the phone.

Maya sat on the floor in her laundry room with her back against the wall, still cradling the phone in her hand. The part of her vision about India hadn't changed, but at the end of the vision she wasn't grieving alone. She saw her parents' faces, the only other people who knew about the secret from her past that was ready to turn her life upside down after twelve years of silence.

Chapter 23

After spending two nights away from home, Antoine felt like a stranger in his own house. He wasn't surprised to find the house sparkling clean as always. India took pride in making sure everything was in its own place. There wasn't a speck of dust clinging to the photos and paintings that adorned the walls in the living room and den. The beds were made in all the bedrooms upstairs and the bathrooms smelled fresh as always, like Pine Sol.

Downstairs in the kitchen he fixed himself a sandwich, again not surprised by the cleanliness that surrounded him. Not one dirty dish rested in the sink or upon the countertops. The table top was free of crumbs and dishes as well. Antoine took a seat in his usual chair at the head of the small table, bringing the beer he'd grabbed from the fridge to rest on a coaster.

He couldn't remember the last time he'd had the house all to himself in the middle of the day. The quietness that surrounded him was almost depressing. He longed for the sounds of his family, sounds from the TV breezing in from the den; the clashing of pots and pans as India prepared to make their family dinner. It was almost funny that he'd taken so much for granted over the years.

India for him was the one, the perfect wife. She'd happily accepted Ariel as a part of their lives and he knew she genuinely loved his daughter and only wanted the best for her. For the first six months the two got along well, and Antoine couldn't have been happier. But his euphoria was soon broadsided by the evil-doings of Rachel. India felt he should straighten her out and set her in her place, but she didn't understand that Rachel was who she'd always been. The person that was changing was India. That's why he was so hard on her, determined to make her understand that somebody else's actions shouldn't change who she was.

Maybe he should've tried harder to make Ariel realize that the things her mother taught her were wrong. It wasn't that he never disciplined Ariel, but he also understood the confusion she must have felt having her mother teach her one way of life and then he and India teaching her a different way of life; what they felt was right. He tried so hard to make India see that despite all the negative things that came from her mouth, Ariel was still just an eight-year-old girl, lost in a world of confusion after being separated from her mother. Sure Rachel was unfit but that didn't change the depth of Ariel's love for her nor the amount of trust she had in her.

After finishing his meal, Antoine made his way back upstairs. He'd left his suitcase by the door in their bedroom. He unpacked the contents of the suitcase, placing everything back in its original place before returning the suitcase to the top shelf of the closet. He sat down on India's side of their bed and grabbed one of her pillows. He brought it to his nose and inhaled her femininity, almost able to taste the green apples and vanilla that clung to his nostrils. He'd tried his best to hate her, hoping that being away from her would lessen the love he carried in the chambers of his heart. Yet the old saying had proven true; absence makes the heart grow fonder.

His back was turned to the door and though he hadn't heard her entrance, the fragrance of green apples and vanilla grew stronger. He turned slowly on the bed and there she stood in the doorway of their bedroom, her face wet with tears yet a smile gracing her beautiful face.

"I know you told me not to come home early, but I had to," she began explaining as she made her way to the bed, taking a seat next to him. "I had lunch with Maya, and she made me promise not to go back to the bank. She's been having these visions and she thinks Mario is going to do something to hurt one of us." India went on to tell him about Maya's visions and her encounter with Mario that morning.

"It sounds like he's got some screws loose for sure," Antoine agreed. "I don't believe much in that psychic shit, but I think it would be best if you stay as far away from his as possible. I don't wanna have to put a cap in his ass, but I will." Actually he did want to put a cap in him; he just didn't want to face the consequences of those actions.

Changing the subject, India asked the obvious question, the one that had been burning her brain since his call to her office. "Have you reached a decision yet? I don't want to rush you, I just, uh, I just need to know where we stand."

He turned to his wife, stared deeply into her hazel eyes just as he'd done on their wedding day and so many times when they'd lost themselves in the ecstasy of their lovemaking. He took her hands in his, "It's going to take some time before I can forgive you, India. But I'm willing to try if you're ready. Are you sure this is what you want? Can you handle loving me and helping me support Ariel as she struggles with all the confusion her mother brings on?"

She nodded yes, but that answer wasn't enough for him. He needed to make sure before they continued. "India, we'll have arguments and disagreements, but I need to know that you're strong enough to hold it together without running to some other man. I can't–" he stopped mid-sentence. "No, I *won't* go through this again. I love you, but if you ever step out on me again, there's no coming back, India. I won't put up with it, and I won't put our kids through it."

Tears raced down her face as they embraced. It felt so good, so natural to be back in his arms. She never wanted to have him leave her side again. With that thought she said, "I'll go in Monday to clean out my office."

"No, I don't want you there without me," Antoine protested. "We don't know what Mario is capable of. After we pick the kids up today, we'll drop them off at your mother's and go by your office. You can fax them your resignation or let them figure it out."

India didn't disagree; she was too happy to have her husband back. Instead she looked at the time on the clock and realized they had an hour and a half to themselves before the kids had to be picked up. Antoine's eyes met hers and with no words spoken between the two they slowly undressed each other before making love, reuniting their bodies as well as their hearts.

Chapter 24

Unable to get any work done, Mario stood, peering out his office window watching people enter and exit the bank. He'd gone back to Sharon's office to see if she wanted to have lunch in the park, but her secretary said she'd left for the day. He tried calling her phone several times but was directed to her voicemail. He didn't know what was going on with her. First she'd tried breaking up with him on her birthday of all days, and now she was avoiding him. He had a good mind to go by her house and straighten things out.

Just as he was about to abandon the window and return to his desk to make yet another call to her, he noticed her in the company of a man, walking toward the bank's entrance. He'd only seen the man in pictures but even from the third floor he could tell that the man was Antoine Joiner, the man who thought he was Sharon's husband.

What the hell is he doing here? Mario wondered. From what she'd told him, the man worked Monday through Friday and some times on Saturdays. He worked as late as seven in the evenings, but here it was not even four o'clock. *And why the hell is he carrying boxes?*

Reaching in his desk drawer, Mario removed his nine-millimeter semi-automatic handgun. He tucked it in the waistband of his pants and buttoned his coat to conceal the weapon. That man was trying to take Sharon away from him and there was no way in hell he was going to let that happen.

"If it's a war he wants, it's a war he'll get," Mario declared as he pushed the down button inside the elevator. He was going to the second floor to reclaim his wife once and for all.

Chapter 25

Teresa smiled when the handsome bank president stepped off the elevator. As always he was wearing an Armani suit and he was wearing it well. She couldn't deny her attraction for the man, but he'd ignored her hopeless flirting, obviously more interested in her married boss. Sure, they tried being discreet, but Teresa was no fool, they were as much an item as Jay-Z and Beyoncé.

Knowing that India was in her office with her husband, she wondered if Mr. Thomas was aware. When he walked toward the closed office door, Teresa quickly abandoned her chair, rushing toward him.

"Ms. Joiner's in with her husband right now, Sir. Is there something I can help you with?" she asked giving him the knowing eye. She wasn't trying to get all up in their business, but she didn't want their drama unfolding right there in the bank.

Mario looked at the young woman, flashing her a seductive smile that caused her to melt like butter. He knew she was attracted to him, but she wasn't his type. He wasn't into blonde headed chicks of any race, especially the ones with blue eyes. In his opinion, she was far from beautiful and wasn't to be compared to one as beautiful as his Sharon.

"Teresa, right?"

She blushed like a small child, thrilled that he remembered her name. She nodded.

"Would you be a dear and take this downstairs to the head teller, please? I forgot to ask Emily to do it this morning," he told her, handing her some papers in an envelope. It wasn't anything pressing, but it would be enough to get her out his way.

"Sure thing, Sir," she eagerly agreed. She walked away with an extra twist of her hips. As she reached the elevators, she couldn't resist looking over her shoulders to see if he was watching. She covered her mouth to cover a schoolgirl giggle when she saw that not only was he looking, he winked at her.

Once the silly girl disappeared behind the steel elevator doors, Mario readjusted the gun in his waist before opening the office door.

Antoine was the first to see him being that India's back was turned. "What the fuck are you doing here?" he snarled.

"I came for my wife," Mario said, resting his hand comfortably on the gun, waiting for just the right moment to whip it out, aim, and fire at his opponent.

Now facing her ex-lover, India shook her head in dismay and spoke slowly and firmly, "I am not your wife. We've been through this once this morning, Mario. I'm not Sharon."

Her words caused sharp pains to shoot through both his head and heart. For a moment, the images before him became distorted, a mere blur. He closed his eyes, blinked rapidly several times, and opened them again. The images were clear now, both were looking at him as if he were a mad man.

He motioned Sharon to come to him. He didn't want her in harm's way when he pulled the gun out. Mario needed his wife standing behind him. "Come to me, Sharon," he said.

Antoine walked closer to the man, taking in his strange behavior, the confused look in his eyes. "Do you not get it? This is my wife and her name ain't Sharon," he said, two inches from Mario's nose.

With a sinister grin, Mario pushed the man backwards and reached for the gun, but before he could pull the gun out, Antoine was in attack mode. His first punch sent Mario flying backwards, falling into the door. Antoine, ignoring his wife's screams, released his anger on the man who'd bedded his wife. Repeatedly he pounded his fists into Mario's face, sending blood and sweat flying throughout the office. It wasn't his intentions to kill the man, but Antoine couldn't stop himself, didn't have the self control to end the assault. It wasn't until security came in and restrained him that the bloody massacre ended.

"Mr. Thomas, Sir, are you okay? Do you need an ambulance?" one of the three guards asked.

Antoine looked down at his victim and felt no remorse when he saw the damage left by his flying fists of fury. The man's bottom lip was cut, and blood spewed from it; fresh blood oozed from both nostrils; and he had a cut over his right eye. His face was badly bruised and if Antoine could have freed himself from the two guards, he would have pounded the flesh from the man's face.

"No," Mario said waving the guard away. "I don't need an ambulance. I just want him out of this building," he said, his cold stare landing on Antoine, who didn't flinch.

"You don't want to press any charges?" the older of the three guards asked. Mr. Thomas, from where he was standing, had taken quite an ass whipping, and the man the other two guards was holding didn't look as if he were done. On the contrary, he looked as if he had a lot more ass whippings to issue out and all of them had Mario Thomas' name written on them.

"Didn't you hear what I said?" Mario asked through clenched teeth. He was now standing, carefully readjusting the gun in his waistband. He couldn't believe no one had seen the weapon during the assault. "I just want this person out of my bank, now."

"Yes, Sir," the older man said, tipping his hat to the bank's president. "Let's get him out of here fellas," he said to his co-workers.

India grabbed the boxes, willing to leave behind whatever she hadn't managed to pack. She would ask Teresa to have the paintings forwarded to her address via a courier service. There was no way she was coming back to the bank, ever. Mario was a nutcase; Maya had been right all along.

"Sharon, baby, where are you going?" Mario asked as India rushed toward the door, behind the guards who were escorting her husband.

Without looking at him, she quickened her pace. He continued to call after her, but she refused to turn around. All she wanted was to get as far away from him as possible.

Teresa was back at her desk now, confused by the scene before her. India's husband was being escorted by three guards, and she was right on their heels carrying boxes. Her eyes were puffy and it was obvious that she'd been crying. Mr. Thomas looked as if he'd been badly beaten and he was calling out to *Sharon*.

Who the hell is Sharon, and what did I miss? Teresa wondered as she sat, mouth wide open, at her desk.

Chapter 26

The events of the day had proven to be a bit much for Antoine. As he lay in bed beside his wife listening to her light snores, he couldn't help wondering if he'd been too hasty in his decision to give their marriage another chance. He knew without doubt that he loved her, but he was angry every time he thought about Mario touching her, kissing her soft lips, and enjoying the essence of her virtue, something promised to him and him alone.

He wanted to kill the man and had the security guards not rushed in when they did, he would have done just that. He couldn't help thinking what would have happened had Jay not told him about the affair. What if he'd seen it for himself, his wife with another man? He kept a gun in his car, and he knew without a second thought that he would have killed the man on the spot.

India, in her slumber, snuggled closer to him, pressing her firm rear end into his groin, breathing life into his manhood. His body wanted her, to explore the soft crevices of her womanly folds. But mentally, mentally he couldn't make love to her because so many thoughts plagued his mind like deadly viruses.

Still restless he squeezed his eyes closed in search of sleep. A good night's sleep would hopefully stop the pounding in his head and the thoughts racing through his mind. As he finally drifted off to that magical dreamland, Antoine began to dream, images of his earlier thoughts coming to life right before his half-closed eyes.

His nose flared and his slightly chiseled jaw flinched as he watched, through narrowed eyes, the couple before him. The woman tilted her head back and he heard her soft, seductive laughter as the man beside her whispered into her ear, words meant to be shared only between the two. He rubbed her hand affectionately, the left hand where her wedding ring rested. They looked like the perfect couple, so happy with each other that they didn't even feel the penetration of his eyes staring through them, burning holes into their flesh.

Antoine wanted to storm over to the table and take what was his, his wife. He had a gun right outside in his car, and thoughts of sticking the barrel of the gun right between Mario Thomas' eyes invaded his psyche. He wanted to pistol whip the man before blowing his brains all over the expensive Italian suit he wore.

And India, he didn't know what he was feeling for her in that moment. She was his wife and even in his moment of rage he loved her. He couldn't imagine himself physically harming her, yet he still wanted her to suffer, some how and some way. She deserved to feel the same sharp pain that cut through his heart like a knife, cutting his life away.

Still unaware of his presence, the couple continued their intimate conversation, sharing kisses and laughter, something Antoine and India had not shared in months. She looked so happy that it caused his breathing to stop momentarily. Another man was making his wife happy, a task that he had obviously failed by India's standard.

Mario gently stroked India's beautiful face, and she looked at him the way she used to look at Antoine, her eyes full of love and passion. It was in that moment that Antoine lost it. He wanted Mario out of their lives, and not just for the night, on the chance that the two of them would continue their sordid affair. Antoine wanted Mario out of the picture completely.

He stormed out of the restaurant, ran to his truck, and opened the glove compartment.

He checked the clip, saw that it was loaded, locked it back in place, and slammed the glove compartment closed. He hurried, feet barely touching the ground as he stormed toward the lobby's entrance.

Antoine closed his eyes and took a deep breath. He had so many thoughts racing through his mind. He wanted to hear the gun explode and see a bullet tear through Mario's skull, causing blood and brain matter to spew everywhere. Just who the fuck did he think he was, messing around with another man's wife just because he was some rich, pretty boy? Antoine wanted to watch the man die, but he really hadn't thought about what would happen next. Antoine hadn't thought about the police taking him away from his family, and the possibility of him having to fight every day for his manhood, as gangster wanna-be booty snatchers tried to take what he'd never give willingly to a man. He'd lose the very thing he thought he was protecting, his family.

Out of nowhere, Jay appeared. "Give me the gun," he demanded, his hand outstretched.Antoine looked toward the glass doors that led to the lobby of The Plaza. His wife was in there, dining with and loving another man. Images of them in more intimate positions flashed through his head, causing his eyes to water. How many times had this man fucked his wife, tasted her sweet nectar, and stroked her soft walls? Had she wrapped her soft, thick lips around his shaft, stroked his head with her tonsils, bringing him to orgasms so intense that his toes curled the same way she did with him? The thought of his wife sucking another man's manhood caused bile to rise in the back of his throat.

"It wasn't supposed to be like this," he told Jay, shaking his head from side to side. "It wasn't supposed to be like this."

Before Jay could answer, Antoine was off and running. He made his way into the restaurant, darting between and leaping over tables until he reached the table shared by his wife and her lover. Both were shocked to see him. Tears sprang from her eyes as she stood, mouth open, words pouring out, but Antoine heard nothing. Without asking any questions, he pointed the gun at Mario's dome, and before the man could blink, a loud explosion rang throughout the restaurant. As if in slow motion, Mario's eyes closed as his body slowly spilled from the chair.

"Antoine, baby, wake up! Wake up!" India was shaking him out of the dream. Slowly he opened his eyes, combed his surroundings, and looked at the clock. It was almost four in the morning. The dream seemed so real; the images, the sounds, the pounding in his chest as he pulled the trigger. He even tasted the bile in his throat, thinking of his wife orally satisfying another man.

"Are you okay? You were talking and swearing in your sleep," she said softly, stroking his bare chest with her fingertips.

"I'm fine," he said, gently pushing her hand away. As much as he loved her, her gentle touch now repulsed him. Getting back on track in their marriage was going to take more hard work than he'd originally gave thought to, and he honestly didn't know if he could ever get past the images of his wife with another man.

Stung by her husband's rejection, India turned on her right side; with her back to him she allowed hot tears to caress her cheeks. She thought everything was fine when they made love earlier that day, but after the fight with Mario, things seemed to take a turn for the worse. *Will he ever truly forgive me?* She wondered.

Chapter 27

I didn't know what to make of my weekend alone with Antoine. He wouldn't touch me and barely spoke two words to me. I kept asking what was bothering him, as if I didn't know, but he wouldn't talk to me. We spent the entire weekend inside, looking at re-runs of *Good Times* on TVLand. When Sunday rolled around I hoped we'd go to church and have dinner with our families but that didn't happen either. We had take-out with JJ, Thelma, Michael, Florida, and James. The Evans' were always cool with me, capable of making the best of a bad situation, but they weren't doing anything to help my marriage. For thirty minutes each episode that family was scratching and surviving; James and Florida Evans weren't having marital problems like India and Antoine Joiner.

Not having a job was taking its toll on me by noon Monday. When the house phone rang I hoped it was Antoine calling on his lunch break, but to my surprise it was my mother. I couldn't remember the last time I'd visited her or even called to say more than "Trey wants to stay with you this weekend." She didn't know about any of the drama with Mario and I wasn't ready to tell her.

At first I just stared at the Caller ID, hoping it would miraculously change. Of course it didn't. *Cassandra Jordan* lit up the display, and she wasn't about to hang up obviously. She'd no doubt called my job and was told I wasn't in or possibly that I had resigned.

On the fifth ring, I picked up just before the answering machine's greeting roared to life. "Hello?"

"And hello to you, too," Momma sang into the receiver. "Why aren't you at work? And why didn't you come to church yesterday? I tried calling but kept getting the machine. We missed you all at dinner. Is everything okay?"

Not one question, no, she had to go for the gusto. "We're fine, Momma," I told my first lie and continued into the second, "I wasn't feeling too well, you know cramps, so we stayed in and just looked at TV. I guess the ringer was off or something." I was pacing the floor, scared shitless, because if my Momma knew or even thought I was lying to her she'd come to my house and whip my ass. That's why I wasn't about to tell her about no damn affair with no crazy ass Mario.

"Oh yeah?" she asked slyly. Was I busted? "Trey told me that Antoine and you had a fight Wednesday, said that Antoine didn't come back home until Friday." Yep, I was cold-busted. "So, I say again, is everything okay?" Momma was elaborating every syllable, letting me know she meant business and daring me to lie to her.

I slumped down on the sofa in our den, grabbed the remote and muted the sound on the television before I answered. "I had an affair, Momma, and somehow Antoine found out. He did leave for a couple days, but he's back now and we're trying to work it out."

"You did what?" It wasn't that she didn't hear me clearly; I was sure she was shocked at my careless behavior, carrying on like some half-raised strumpet.

I gave Momma the low down on my affair and all the drama that had transpired. I conjured up some tears to lessen the threat of her coming over with her belt. The strain on my marriage was whipping me badly enough already. I didn't need Momma swinging her belt across my backside.

"I don't know personally, but I can imagine it is hard raising another woman's child, especially when the likes of Rachel is involved. But still, India, that doesn't entitle you to an affair. Don't you know the risks of contracting STD's, AIDS, or getting pregnant and not knowing just who the child's father is?" I was about to remind my mother that I was smart enough to use condoms, but she must've been reading my mind. "And don't give me no lame answer about condoms because we all know they're not a free pass to have sex either. They can and have been known to break. Then what? Huh? You're just stuck in a hole that you dug, and the first name you call is God's, the name you should've been calling on all along."

Momma rallied on for about twenty more minutes, crawling up one side and down the other side of my ass. By the time she was done with me, I felt like a ten-year-old girl who'd been punished and ordered to stand with her nose in the corner, on one leg. And there I was a few weeks ago, smiling, glad to be that man's whore. Proud to have him turn me out then but so ashamed when my momma got through with me. Well, almost through with me; Momma wasn't done yet.

"And now you say this man is calling you by his dead wife's name? What's wrong with him? Is he on medication? It sounds like he needs to be," she ranted.

"It was weird, Momma. At first I thought he was just lonely, missing his wife on her birthday, but then he tried to make me believe that I was Sharon. He said we were close to having our life together back." The thought of that conversation made the hairs on the back of my neck stand up.

"Well it sounds like you need to stay far away from this man. Make sure you keep your doors and windows locked, and if you hear anything strange call me and then the police. I'd say call them first but they'll have you on hold so long. Shoot, I'll be at your house opening up a can of whip-ass before the police even get in their cars." Momma laughed. "And baby, you know I'm praying for you and Antoine, as well as Ariel. As hard as it may be to believe, that child is confused to the point that it ain't even funny. You and Ric were blessed to have a good mother growing up, but not every child is as fortunate. Despite the way your daddy broke my heart, I never taught you two to hate that man. No matter what, he'll always be your father, and you owe him respect for that reason alone."

I wasn't going to get into that dogfight so I just agreed with Momma and happily ended the conversation after I convinced her that every door and window were locked. After I placed the phone back on its base, I picked up the remote and turned the sound back up on my favorite TV show, *Girlfriends.* I lost myself in the drama that only Joan, Toni, Maya, and Lyn could create for themselves. As I laughed with them and at them, I pushed all thoughts of my deadbeat dad, crazy ex-lover, and even my struggling marriage to the back of my mind.

Chapter 28

Cassandra Jordan sat on the padded stool before her white baby grand piano. As her fingers gently stroked the ebony and ivory keys, tears filled her eyes. She'd been unaware that she'd been playing *Save the Best for Last,* her wedding song. Memories of Myles filled her head and her heart as tears trickled down her still beautiful, yet slowly aging face.

Cassandra tried to suppress the painful memories, but the night she lost Myles was one that would not flee her memories. Though she was strong most days, there were moments when the events from five years earlier resurfaced, bringing the pain back as if she were losing her husband all over again. She could still hear the loud impact, metal twisting, glass breaking, and tires squealing as the driver raced away from the scene. Those sounds had brought Cassandra sprinting out the front door. Before she even saw the scene, the pain in her heart told her it was Myles, and sure enough she opened the front door to see his brand new Lexus coupe completely dismantled. She only caught the tail lights of the other vehicle before it disappeared at the next intersection, taking a left on two tires.

She tried with all her might to open the driver's side door and free her husband from the wreckage but the door, a crumpled, folded mass of fiberglass, wouldn't move. She climbed in on the passenger side of the vehicle. There was no way to move him. His legs were crushed beneath the steering wheel and dashboard; his head lay forward on the deployed airbag; there was blood everywhere.

"Myles! Myles, baby wake up!" she remembered crying out repeatedly as she threw her arms around him, trying to love him back to life. His eyes were open, but he never responded. His breathing was slow and ragged as blood continued to trickle from his many abrasions. As she stared helplessly into his eyes, Cassandra could literally see his transformation from life to death; mortality to spirituality. Neighbors filed out of their houses, assuring her that help was on the way. Some tried to aide Myles, but she cried for them to let her have those final moments with her husband. There was nothing they could've done at that point. God had already sent his angels of mercy; Cassandra felt their peaceful presence as a still coolness lingered around Myles and her. In her arms, Myles Jordan died just moments before the police and paramedics appeared on scene.

There were days when she didn't think she could go on. For weeks she lived in denial, refusing to accept that he, her husband, lover, protector, and best friend, was gone. She still fixed his favorite meals every evening and sat waiting for him to come waltzing through the door. She called his cell phone just to hear the sound of his recorded voice. At night, Cassandra cuddled up with Myles' favorite pair of silk pajamas, inhaling his masculinity, as she cried herself to sleep. Without her children and God Almighty, she never would have climbed out of that hole of depression. Having India and Ric's love and faith in God made all the difference.

That's why she couldn't rest until things were back to normal between India and Antoine. She knew the love between her daughter and son-in-law was as pure as the love she'd shared with Myles. The two of them needed each other like humans need water and air to survive, like humanity needs God, even though some of them don't realize it. Despite India's affair, Cassandra didn't doubt that her daughter was still very much in love with Antoine Joiner.

Antoine had been the one to love India beyond the pain of the broken heart she suffered at the hands of Terrance, Trey's no accounting father. Cassandra had warned India that Terrance was no good but being the naïve teen she was India still fell head over heels in love with him, giving him her virginity. No sooner than she told him of her pregnancy, Terrance was ready to just be friends, something he should have tried before sex.

Picking up the phone, Cassandra dialed Antoine's number. She knew he was at work but maybe he had a few minutes to spare for his mother-in-law.

"Hello, Antoine Joiner, how can I help you?"

Cassandra beamed with pride. He'd finally worked his way up to management and she was so very proud of him. He was more like a son than a son-in-law, always respectful and willing to do anything she asked of him. She hoped he would hear her out today.

"Well, Mr. Joiner, hello," she greeted. "This is your lovely mother-in-law. How are you?"

Antoine couldn't hide the smile that covered his face at the sound of Cassandra's voice. Unlike most mother-in-laws, his was pretty cool.

"How are you? It's good to hear from you," he replied, as they continued the formalities, talking about the weather, his promotion, and everything except the real reason for Cassandra's call.

She finally got to the point. "Ant, you know I've always stayed out of you and India's personal affairs over the years," she said, taking a deep breath before she treaded into deep waters. "And I don't want to overstep my boundaries now, but I have to speak my peace."

"I guess you know about the affair," Antoine said, his smile disappearing. It wasn't his favorite subject to discuss. He thought about it enough; talking about it only added to his array of emotions.

"I talked to India earlier. I knew there was some reason why she'd been avoiding me. Antoine, she's my daughter and I love her, but I can not and will not uphold her in her wrong doing. No matter how stressful things were between the two of you, an affair shouldn't have been her way of dealing with the situation. And now I understand this man is causing so many problems that she's had to quit her job because he thinks she's his dead wife—just a lot of unnecessary drama," Cassandra said. She was now outside on her patio, enjoying the beautiful spring breeze, birds chirping, and beautiful flowers in bloom.

Antoine didn't interrupt; he just listened to his mother-in-law as she continued. "I'm concerned about what this man may be capable of, but India is more concerned that you can't forgive her. She thinks she's lost you, Antoine, but I hope that's not true."

Finally Antoine spoke, "Cassandra, I really don't know what to do. I know I love my wife, but I can't stop thinking about her being with another man. I thought I could handle it, but maybe I went back home too soon. I just don't know." He was staring at a picture of India and him that rested on top of his small desk. It was taken shortly after they were married, long before the drama with Rachel and the affair that threatened to tear them apart.

"I understand that. I just hope that you'll at least try, Antoine.

You and India remind me so much of Myles and me. That's the kind of love you hold on to, the kind of love that lives on beyond even death," she said as she choked back tears. "If you love my daughter as much as I'm sure you do, hold on tight to her, baby, and don't ever let that love go."

Antoine hung up the phone after saying goodbye to Cassandra. He thought about all the different emotions he was dealing with, trying to put them in perspective. No matter how many negative images clouded his psyche, he knew, without doubt that he still loved India. He couldn't imagine his life without her.

He picked up the phone and dialed his home number. His wife answered on the second ring. "Hey, I was thinking, maybe we can go out Friday night. You know, just the two of us," he said. It was a step.

Chapter 29

Mario had a stop to make before he went home. He'd been watching Sharon all week, waiting for the right moment to reclaim her. He tailed her from afar when she drove the kids to school and on her way back to the house before he drove to the bank. He spent evenings watching their home, waiting for just the two of them, her and that Antoine clown to leave the house together. Mario wanted to reclaim his wife but first he had to claim the other man's life, making sure that he wouldn't cause trouble for them ever again.

Mario pulled into the parking lot at a nearby Wal Mart, parking his silver Lexus next to a white SUV. He paid no attention to the lady in the driver's seat; didn't even notice how intensely she watched him as he hurried into the store.

Maya had already made her purchases and was preparing to leave the store when none other than Mario Thomas pulled his shiny whip into the parking space beside her. She watched him as he, dressed in a green Italian suit, made his way toward the entrance and decided to see what he was up to. She jumped out of her vehicle and hurried into the store behind him.

From aisle to aisle, Maya tailed him, ducking out of sight to make sure she went unnoticed. He bought duct tape, bottled water, and other odds and ends. When he made his way to the register, she decided to make her presence known. She picked up a magazine for checkout. She needed some reason to be in the line.

"Excuse me," she said. Mario turned to face her, a blank expression on his face. The two had only met once when she came to the bank to have lunch with India. He'd been leaving her office when Maya was coming in. "I don't know if you remember me, but I'm a friend of India's." She extended her right hand. "Maya."

He took her hand, shaking it very briefly before saying, "Sorry, I don't recall." The woman, though very beautiful, bore no familiarity. Her full figured physique, uniquely beautiful eyes, and silky, jet black hair, rang no bells for him. Besides, he knew no one named India.

His touch left Maya cold and speechless. In those few seconds of contact, she saw a scene from his past flash before her eyes. She saw those same cold, green eyes, only the face was younger; maybe that of a teenager. Mario stood in a room surrounded by three hanging bodies, a man, a woman, and a young boy—all three of their faces bore resemblance to his own. There was no pain or regret in his eyes, just a cold hatred.

Chills shot up and down Maya's spine as she realized just how Mario had severed all ties with his family; he'd murdered them! Dropping the magazine to the floor, she stumbled backwards, claiming distance between herself and the murderer. After bumping into several people, she finally made her way to the entrance where she bolted toward her vehicle.

Mario watched the crazy woman run from the store and shook his head. Maybe Dr. Martin should have been trying to contact her because she was obviously in need of therapy. One minute she was talking normally and in the next second she was running away in a panic for no obvious reason.

After paying for his merchandise, Mario hurried to his car. He was going to check by Sharon's to see if there was any activity before he went home. He checked his glove compartment to make sure his gun was in place. Seeing that it was, he pulled out of the parking lot, hoping that he'd soon be able to tie up those nagging loose ends.

Chapter 30

I was glowing, smiling from ear to ear when I picked the kids up from school Friday. They'd barely climbed in and buckled up before I said, "Guess what?" peering at them through the review mirror. My smile was as wide as the Mississippi is long.

"What?" they both asked in unison, seemingly intrigued by my happiness. I hadn't had a whole lot to smile about recently, but today was a new day.

"You two are going to visit Grandma Cassandra while Daddy and I go out to dinner." I was like a big-boned sister in a size-five mini skirt, about to burst at the seams. They both cheered and I couldn't help but be thankful. Only God Himself could have repaired the relationship with Ariel and me, and we were definitely on the right track.

Momma was as excited as the kids and me when I told her of the dinner plans Antoine was arranging for us. I spent some time with her and the kids before I headed home, giving myself just enough time to get beautiful for my handsome husband.

My cell phone rang just as I entered my subdivision. Caller ID revealed that it was Maya.

I couldn't wait to tell her about my planned evening. I had a great feeling that things were going to be okay between Antoine and me.

"Girl, guess what?" I answered, still floating on my natural high.

"I'm in your driveway, where are you?" she responded in a panicked voice.

"I'm pulling up now," I said, noticing the big, white SUV as I rounded the corner. "What's wrong?"

"I see you," she answered, exiting her vehicle. She waved before hanging up, waiting for me to park so we could talk face to face.

I was barely parked before Maya had my door open, practically dragging me out of the vehicle before I killed the engine. "Girl, what the hell is going on?" I asked. She looked like she'd just seen a ghost; her face was white as a sheet.

"He killed them, India. I saw it when I shook his hand today; he killed them. And he was buying tape and stuff at Wal Mart. I don't know what he's gonna do." Tears rolled down her face. "Oh God, I'm so scared for you, India!"

I barely understood a word she said and what I did understand audibly didn't make any sense at all. "What are you talking about? Who killed them? And who is them?"

Maya looked up and down the street, as if she thought I had been followed. She was definitely badly shaken up over something. She ushered me toward the door, still looking over her shoulder.

Inside the kitchen, she locked both locks on the door and peered out the window. She was scaring the shit out of me. My eyes watered and my mouth felt dry. I felt my bones rattle as I shook like a leaf on a tree. When Maya finally told me about her encounter with Mario and what she'd seen, I nearly emptied my bladder in the middle of my kitchen. Mario had finally stopped calling and texting me. I was convinced that everything was finally over after that day in my office.

"He's up to something, India. I got this feeling that something really bad is about to happen and I'm so scared," Maya cried, throwing her arms around me.

It was at that moment that I heard Antoine pull into the garage. I pulled away from Maya. "Maya, please don't mention a word of this to Antoine," I pleaded. I didn't want anything to ruin our evening.

Maya stared intently at me, her look one of total dismay. "Maya, we're going out tonight, and I hope this means we're on our way to leaving the past behind us. The last thing he wants to hear right now is anything about Mario."

The locks clicked on the door and my eyes begged Maya to get it together before Antoine walked in. She silently nodded, though I knew she didn't agree with not telling him just how dangerous Mario was.

"What's up, Maya?" Antoine asked when he walked in. He kissed her cheek before pulling me close to him and tenderly kissing my forehead. "Let me guess, India called you over here to help her get ready for tonight."

"Busted." Maya laughed nervously. "If I don't help her, y'all will never get there on time." That said, we rushed upstairs to get me ready for a romantic evening with my husband. As far as I was concerned, the conversation about Mario was over. He was a part of my past and my only focus that evening was my husband and our future.

Chapter 31

Mario watched as the driver in the SUV passed by him; it was the crazy lady that had run out the store after introducing herself to him. He wondered how she knew Sharon and why she'd been visiting. Her vehicle had been there when he pulled up, but he didn't see her exit, only her entrance moments before she passed him. He'd also seen that Antoine guy pull into the garage in that hooptie Caprice. That guy was all wrong for Sharon, definitely not her type. His Sharon loved classy guys, like himself.

He watched the SUV until it was out of sight, smiling to himself that he'd gone unnoticed. His car was in the garage of one of the vacant houses just down the street from Sharon, hidden beneath a car cover. He was hidden in the neatly trimmed shrubbery with a pair of binoculars. Lucky for him there were a few vacant houses that sat together and a house occupied by an older couple just down the street, but they apparently hadn't noticed his daily routine.

Just as he turned his attention back to Sharon's house, he noticed her baby blue BMW backing out into the roadway. With the aide of his binoculars he could see that she was not alone; Antoine was behind the wheel. As soon as the car passed the house, he hurried to his car, removed the cover, and sped away, determined not to lose them. The time had finally come.

Chapter 32

Antoine could barely keep his eyes off India as they drove toward one of her favorite restaurants, The Italian Grill. She had her hair in an upsweep, soft curls resting around the crown of her head. He wanted to kiss her fire red lips and rip the red and white dress from her soft skin.

India couldn't stop blushing when she noticed the look of longing in her husband's eyes. Maya had done wonders with her hair and makeup. Of course they hadn't agreed on the dress, Maya thinking it was a bit much for The Italian Grill, but India wouldn't cave. She knew how much Antoine liked seeing her in that dress. It fit her curves like a glove and he couldn't keep his eyes nor his hands off her.

She eyed him and smiled approvingly. Though dressed more casually than she, he was looking good in his khaki Dockers and a navy polo-type, Dockers shirt. He had a fresh haircut and shave, and he smelled good enough to bite into. They had yet to have dinner and there they both were already looking forward to dessert.

Antoine parked the car, but left the radio on, enjoying the latest Usher hit. He took India's hands in his before pulling her forward for a kiss. He couldn't sit through dinner without tasting her sweet lips first, knowing he'd taste more once they were back home. As always she melted into him, pouring all her love for him into a kiss that left them both smiling and panting, desiring more.

As they exited the car, neither noticed the silver Lexus that whipped into the parking lot. Antoine reached for India's hand as they walked toward the entrance.

"Sharon!" Both turned at the sound of the all too familiar voice. The sight of Mario snapped them out of their state of bliss. Antoine walked toward the man, prepared for another fist fight but without warning, Mario pulled out a gun, stopping Antoine dead in his tracks. A sinister grin teased his lips and without a word, Mario aimed at his target and pulled the trigger. Screaming to the top of her lungs, India fell to her knees in a puddle of blood.

Chapter 33

Everything had happened so fast. The lights were blinding me. The sirens had deafened me. I felt the hot, sticky blood on my hands and face. There was so much blood! *Oh my God! Antoine!* I heard my own voice in my head. *Does anyone else hear me?*

"Antoine," I screamed as I fell to the ground.

"Mrs. Joiner? Mrs. Joiner, are you okay?" a deep voice asked repeatedly.

My mouth was still open, but I couldn't find the words. I heard myself gasping for breath. I felt hot tears streaming down my face. There was a tightening pain in my stomach.

After several moments, I finally managed to ask, "How is my husband? Where is he?"

A short, stout black officer helped pull me back to my feet. My head was spinning. My stomach was weak. He wrapped his arms around my shoulders when my knees buckled and threatened to send me crashing back to the pavement.

"Do you need to sit for a moment longer?" he asked gently.

I shook my head no and said, "Take me to my husband. I need to see my husband."

"Mrs. Joiner, they are doing all they can for your husband. He's in bad shape."

"Sir, please, take me to my husband!" I knew he was in bad shape. I saw all the blood that oozed from his body. I covered his wound with one hand while holding him close with my free arm until help arrived. Then he was taken away by the paramedics while I was questioned by the police.

The expression on the officer's face told me that he didn't want to take me to Antoine, but he knew by my expression that I was persistent. Reluctantly, he escorted me to the ambulance where Antoine was. There were three paramedics frantically working on him.

"This is Mrs. Joiner. She's the victim's wife," the officer explained.

"Your husband has lost a lot of blood. His blood pressure has dropped tremendously. We have to get him to the hospital right now," said one of the paramedics.

Before I could utter a response, I was assisted into the ambulance. Antoine was not moving, but I could hear him breathing. His eyes were open and I looked into those eyes and said, "I love you." He stared back at me and despite my fear I tried to smile at him. His eyes closed and one of the paramedics screamed, "Full code! Full code!"

It's the last thing I remembered before falling to the floor of the ambulance.

Chapter 34

Mario was only able to carry out part of his plan, shooting Antoine. He'd tried to grab Sharon but after the gunfire and her gut-wrenching screams, people, potential witnesses had come running out of the restaurant. Hearing sirens in the distance, Mario had to flee the scene without his beloved Sharon.

He was disappointed that he'd have to wait a little longer to get her back but being that things didn't look good for Antoine that brought a smile to Mario's face. He lost a lot of blood, and Mario was sure that he'd die, leaving him the victor to reclaim his Sharon and live happily ever after.

Having to lie low in case the police were looking for him, Mario paced the floor of a cheap hotel waiting for his wife to call him or walk in the front door. He was ready to celebrate the death of Antoine Joiner and live happily ever after with Sharon again. This time they'd be together, forever, and he'd see to that, even if it meant killing her and then himself.

Chapter 35

Somehow I made all the phone calls. Beverly didn't have any transportation, so my mother was picking her up. Jay was out of town but would be driving like a bat out of hell to get there. Maya was on her way as well.

Momma and Beverly arrived first with Lisa and Annette in tow. The two already had no love for me, and I knew there would be drama. As much as they hated me, I knew they loved their brother. Just as I expected they rushed right over to where I was sitting and lit in on me.

"Why you do this to Antoine?" Annette asked, smelling like a fresh joint.

"I didn't…"

"Don't lie! You shot him! You shot my brother!" Lisa yelled. "I knew she was a gold digger, trying to kill my brother for insurance money, no doubt."

"Damn all that," Annette yelled, boldly pointing her finger in my face. "We gone beat this ho's ass! She ain't getting away with shooting my damn brother!"

"Hold up," Momma yelled as she positioned herself between Annette and me. Normally I'd be up for the fight, but tonight I felt guilty about all that had happened. I didn't shoot Antoine, but were it not for my affair with Mario he wouldn't have been fighting for his life.

"Ain't no hold up," Lisa screamed as she snatched her large hoop earrings off. Beverly ran over to stand in front of her, trying to restore peace. Still I just sat there, too consumed with guilt to even stand up and defend myself. On some level I felt their anger toward me and their discontent for me was justified. It was the one and only time they would get away with calling me out of my name and accusing me of something as lame as killing my husband for insurance money.

"What's this all about?" Maya asked as she rushed in from the main entrance. She wasn't one for drama, but that night, she looked like she was ready for whatever. Security came running from another direction and the two big men took control of the situation.

"What's going on?" the shorter one asked. He reminded me of actor, Michael Jai White; down to the Mohawk he sported.

Annette pointed at me and screamed, "Arrest her! She tried to kill my brother!" Tears streamed down my face. I finally opened my mouth to speak in an effort to defend myself, but no words came. I wanted to tell the security officers that I would never try to kill my husband; I loved my husband. But the harder I tried to speak, the more difficult the task became. Momma and Ms. Beverly ended up explaining, as best they could, what really happened. They knew Antoine had been shot and that the police were searching high and low for the suspect. Momma knew about Mario, but Ms. Beverly didn't as far as I knew. His name wasn't mentioned.

"It's still her fault!" Annette charged toward me like an angry bull. One of the big men grabbed her, lifting her off the ground. She fought wildly, hands swinging and feet kicking in the air, trying to get to me. Lisa took a swing at the security guard who held her sister and they both ended up being carried out the main entrance, spewing venom with every obscenity they hurled in my direction.

"Let's get some coffee, Cassandra," Beverly suggested when she saw the pain in my eyes. My mother was hesitant at first, but Beverly gently pulled her along, knowing that Maya would take care of me. The two mothers made their way down the corridor toward the snack room, leaving their children's drama behind them.

Maya sat next to me. "How you holding up?" she asked, taking my trembling hands into hers.

I took a deep breath and gave Maya the details of our horrible night, a night I'd hope would be the start of a new beginning for my husband and me. I told her how Mario came out of nowhere with the gun, shooting Antoine down like he was an animal. "There were so many cars with lights and sirens wailing. I couldn't see clearly. I couldn't hear anything for the sirens. I couldn't even think straight." I choked back tears before continuing. "But a nice officer came over to me. He didn't want me to see Antoine because of his condition, but he took me to him anyway. We made it here and I called all of you."

"And it's going to be okay," Maya whispered reassuringly.

"I don't know, Maya. He's still out there somewhere. Mario's still out there. How do we know he won't come back and finish Antoine off?" I cried hysterically, not caring about the whispers from the other parties in the lobby.

"Take my hand, India. Take my hand." I did as I was instructed, placing my hand in hers. I listened to her pray for my husband and I closed my eyes and began to pray with her. I didn't know if God listened to wives who cheated on their husbands but still I prayed, hoping he'd have mercy on me just the same.

"Excuse me."

I looked up to see a doctor standing in front of us. She was an older black woman with smooth mahogany skin and brown eyes. The name tag on her white jacket read Dr. Ford.

"Are you family members of Antoine Joiner?" she asked once she saw she had our undivided attention.

Even though my legs felt like gelatin, I quickly rose to my feet. "I...I'm his wife. I'm India Joiner. How is my husband? Can I see him?" Maya stood with me and wrapped her arms around my trembling body for support.

Momma and Beverly returned with their coffee and stood next to Maya and me. Momma held Beverly's hand in hers as we waited for the news.

"He's going to pull through," the doctor announced. We all exhaled and thanked God. "He's lost a lot of blood, but we're going to do a transfusion."

"Who's blood are you giving him?" Beverly asked. In this day of AIDS and hepatitis, everyone was nervous at the mention of transfusions and blood in the same sentence.

"It's his blood, Ma'am. He has made recent donations and we're able to use it." She paused to make sure there were no more questions just yet. "He also has a lot of damage to his appendix. The bullet caused it to rupture. We are going to go ahead and remove it."

"Is that it?" I asked, somewhat relieved. After seeing how much blood he'd lost, I was sure the damages were far worse than a ruptured appendix.

She smiled and said, "That's it. He's going to be just fine and back at home in less than a week."

"Thank God!" He heard our prayers. Even in my darkest hour of shame, God heard my cries and He answered my prayers. "Can I see him now?"

"Actually, he's asked only to see Beverly Joiner, his mother, right now," she replied. I sensed her awkwardness and I was sure she wondered why he wouldn't want to see his wife.

Beverly handed Momma the cup of coffee she was holding. She looked at me, and I tried to hide my disappointment with a smile. It was so hard to smile though because my heart was continuously breaking.

"I'll talk to him," she promised as she joined Dr. Ford. The two women disappeared around a corner at the end of the long corridor.

I flopped back down in the chair and covered my face with my hands because again tears were flooding my face. At that point I couldn't believe I wasn't dehydrated after shedding so many tears.

"Just give him some time, India. Everything is going to be fine." Maya rubbed my back, but neither her words nor her actions did much to soothe the pain I was feeling. "The most important thing is that he's okay. He's going to pull through."

"And until they catch that crazy Mario, you're going to stay with me," Momma added. "I didn't tell Beverly what was going on because I didn't feel it was my place. At some point, the truth is going to come out though. No matter what happens, I'm on your side, baby."

"Thanks, Momma, but I'm not leaving this hospital until I see my husband," I said matter-of-factly. I was as stubborn as him and determined to sit right there until he changed his mind.

Chapter 36

A single man in his early fifties, Timothy Martin lived alone. He positioned himself in his old recliner until he was comfortably inclined, his head resting on a pillow. He'd been watching his favorite television show, *Matlock*, but now it was eleven o'clock, time for the late night news. He aimed the remote at his plasma television and changed the channel to the local news.

The first story was one they'd been running for a few nights. Someone, probably teens, had been vandalizing local churches in Tift and surrounding counties. He often wondered what happened to people where ethics were concerned. Churches were sacred and anyone who would deface a church had to be mentally disturbed.

The second story they ran, however, did grab his attention. He shot straight up in his recliner, both legs now planted firmly on the plush carpet, positioned on either side of the recliner's foot rest. He used the remote to pump up the television's sound.

"In other news, Cordele authorities are searching for a man involved in a near-fatal shooting," the blonde headed reporter announced as a photo appeared on the screen. "This man, Mario Thomas, a former Tift County resident, allegedly opened fire, shooting Antoine Joiner earlier this evening at The Italian Grill in Cordele. Witnesses say Thomas fled the scene just before officers arrived. He is said to be driving a 2006 silver Lexus with GA tag, *Mary, Tom, Henry, Nora, Ida, Charles.* The vehicle and suspect were last seen speeding out The Italian Grill parking lot, traveling west bound on GA 30. Joiner was said to be in critical condition at the scene. As of this broadcast we have no further updates but will keep you informed as new information becomes available."

Who is Antoine Joiner, he wondered. *And how did he cross paths with Mario?* There was not a doubt in Timothy's mind that there was a woman involved, a woman that Mario had no doubt obsessed over, insisting that she was his late wife, Sharon. Obviously Mario fled the scene alone, so whoever the woman was, she'd best be careful because Mario would be back.

The anchorwoman went into another story, but Timothy didn't hear a word. In fact he muted the sound on his television, replaying her earlier broadcast over and over in his mind. He'd known something like this would happen, but until there was a crime committed he couldn't go to the police. Until that night Mario had done nothing illegal even though Timothy strongly suspected he was a danger to himself and others. Now that there was an open case, he was going to call the police and let them know what kind of man they were searching for, a very dangerous one.

Chapter 37

The local news stations had been broadcasting Antoine's near-fatal shooting since the night before. His condition was now stable, but there was no update on the whereabouts of Mario Thomas. Police, however, had been advised by an unnamed, yet reliable source that Mario Thomas suffered from severe depression and had not taken his medication in months. He was considered to be armed, mentally unstable, and extremely dangerous.

Maya worried for India. She felt that Mario would be back; he wouldn't stop until he had what he wanted, India.

Sighing deeply, Maya turned off the television and sorted through the mail. She stacked the bills in one pile and the junk mail in a to-be-shredded pile. Tony would pay the bills late Saturday or early Sunday morning, a task Maya didn't miss. Since the birth of their oldest son, she hadn't worked and he'd insisted on balancing the checkbook. Trusting her husband completely, Maya had no problem with that. Tony was fair, as always, with the money; besides she had her own money, being a sales consultant for Mary Kay. It gave her something to do during the day besides sitting around the house going crazy after completing household chores in the span of two to three hours.

When she came to the last piece of mail in the stack, Maya dropped the lilac colored envelope down on the table and covered her mouth as she gasped. For a few moments she sat, her entire body trembling as she stared down at the envelope and its return address. Finally, she picked it up, hands still shaking profusely, and opened the envelope. Through tear-filled eyes she read the neatly, handwritten words.

Dearest Maya,

I pray that this letter finds you in good health. I know we agreed to never speak again, but it is most urgent that I hear back from you. I know you probably have a busy schedule, but time is of the essence. Please contact me immediately to arrange a meeting. Camille's future lies in the balance.

Sincerely,

Aunt Shelly

Maya continued to reread the words as tears spilled over the paper. The paper absorbed only a small portion of the pain she felt. Her heart raced and her head began to ache as memories from years ago flooded her mind.

She looked up on the wall at her phone, trying to decide if she should pick it up and dial Aunt Shelly's number. She knew she needed to find out what was going on, especially where Camille was concerned. She needed to, but she was terrified of what her aunt's urgent need to talk to her could mean for her future. No one, other than her parents, knew about Camille. What would Tony think when he found out the truth about his perfect wife?

She knew the letter had something to do with her vision, the vision of her dressed in all black, grieving. Was she about to lose Camille all over again?

Chapter 38

Beverly wasn't prepared to hear the news Antoine laid on her. She never would've guessed that India would have an affair, an affair that led to her son being shot. She wasn't quite sure how to feel about the situation. Even though her daughters had always disliked India, claiming she thought she was so much better than everyone else, Beverly had maintained a strong, mother-daughter type relationship with her son's wife. She knew, without an ounce of doubt, that India loved Antoine just as deeply as Antoine loved her. And Beverly especially applauded India for loving Ariel, even in spite of Rachel's constant interference.

She didn't say much to him after he told her what happened. He had to be wheeled into surgery, and she honestly didn't know what to say to him nor India. But after sleeping on it that night and praying about it, Beverly went in to see her son the following day.

"How you doing, son?" she asked as she leaned over to kiss his cheek.

"I'm doing good, Ma. How about you?" He surely sounded stronger than the night before. Beverly knew he would be okay physically, but she worried about him emotionally.

She responded with a smirk and shrug of her shoulders while lowering her heavy frame into a chair at his bedside. "India's been here all night and all morning. Are you going to see her?"

Antoine lowered his eyes and turned his head slightly, not wanting his mother to see the pain in his eyes at the mention of his wife's name. He was all set to put their past behind them when Mario came out of nowhere with that gun, shooting him down in cold blood. The man wanted him dead, and it was only by the grace of God that he was still breathing. In his heart he knew India wasn't responsible for the man's actions, but a part of him still blamed her for getting involved with Mario. Every time he was ready to move forward that man reared his head, coming between them yet again.

Beverly leaned over, gently but firmly grasped her son's handsome face with her hands, hands of a woman who'd worked hard her entire life, and forced him to look at her while she spoke to him. "Son, that girl loves you. I know what she did was wrong, but she still loves you. I see it in her eyes, hear it in her voice, and I feel it in her spirit, Antoine. She loves you the same way I loved your father." The mention of her late husband made Beverly pause momentarily trying not to think about the abuse she'd suffered at that man's hands. Antoine felt her pain, for he, too had been a victim of his father's abuse.

"Ma," he said softly, pulling her back to reality. "Don't–"

She put her hand up, signaling for him to be quiet. "I'm okay," she assured him before continuing. "I know you're not like your father, thank God. You love India a lot more than your father was ever able to love me. Forgive her, son, because if you don't, you'll never forgive yourself for letting her go."

Beverly kissed her son and quietly left his room, not needing a response from him. She left him to his thoughts, trusting that he would make the right decision.

In the lobby, she found her daughter-in-law nursing a cup of coffee. Cassandra had been able to drag India away from the hospital long enough to shower, change clothes, and pick up her car from the shooting scene. She refused to eat much of anything, only drinking coffee in an effort to stay alert in case Antoine wanted to see her. Beverly stared at her, taking in the disheveled ponytail that replaced the upsweep from the night before, the bags under her tired eyes, and her crumpled composure. She looked as though she'd aged five years in less than twenty-four hours.

Sitting next to her, Beverly gently touched India's shoulder. She looked up, trying to force a convincing smile but nothing could hide the gut-wrenching pain she was feeling.

"I take it he's still not ready to see me," India almost whispered.

Beverly slowly shook her head no. "India, he told me about the affair, and I want you to know that I'm not taking sides," Beverly said, holding India's hand in hers. "I can see that you love my son very deeply. I felt that the first time I met you and in spite of everything that's happened recently, I still feel that in my spirit." She squeezed India's hands reassuringly. "I've talked to him, so, let's give him time to think about everything. I'm sure he'll come around."

"Thank you, Beverly," India said, leaning over and hugging her mother-in-law. "I'm going to wait right here."

"Baby, you've got to get some rest. How about you get a good night's sleep and come back in the morning," Beverly reasoned.

Though hesitant at first, India finally agreed. She'd wait a few more hours to see if he asked for her; if not, she would go home and search for sleep within the comforts of her satin sheets.

Chapter 39

Jay walked into the lobby and immediately his eyes landed on his best friend's wife. It was his first time seeing her since telling Antoine about the affair. He could hardly believe his eyes; India, always beautiful, poised, and confident, sat there looking so out of character. Her long hair was normally styled but today it rested, lifelessly, in a ponytail pulled away from her face, which mirrored the pain she was obviously feeling. India's slender fingers trembled as she struggled to hold the Styrofoam cup steady, protecting her body from the steaming contents.

Jay cleared his throat when he approached her. Startled, she turned to face him, apparently tearing herself away from deep thoughts. Her lips curled upward in a tiny smile and she stood, giving him a warm hug.

"Jay, how are you?"

"The better question is how are you?" he asked as their embrace ended.

Shrugging before settling back down in her chair, in a small voice, India answered, "I'm here."

Jay saw her eyes fill with tears and the trembling in her hands attacked the rest of her body. He gently removed the cup of coffee from her hands and set it on the table in front of them. Turning toward her, he pulled her into him in an embrace, allowing her to cry on his shoulders.

He was so overcome with guilt that he almost shed tears as well. An internal battle raged within him to tell her or not tell her. He'd been debating the issue since he learned of the shooting, even more so when he saw Antoine that night after he came out of surgery. A part of him felt responsible; maybe he shouldn't have told Antoine. His friend wouldn't be in the hospital and India wouldn't be the basket case that he cradled in his arms like a baby.

India sniffled, trying to regain her composure; slowly, she pulled away from Jay, assuring him that she was okay.

"How is he doing today?" Jay asked her.

"Ms. Beverly says he looks much better. He should be going home any day now," she answered, between sniffles. Again, she tried to smile, but there was too much pain, too much heartache and guilt. "He still won't see me, Jay."

"I'm sorry to hear that," Jay replied. *Should I tell her,* he pondered.

"It's my own fault. I brought it on myself. I don't know what the hell I was thinking getting involved with another man. I was so stupid, Jay. I was so stupid." She broke down once more and he knew he had to tell her. Maybe it would relieve some of the pain and guilt that she was feeling.

"India, I feel just as guilty," he began, an audible tremble in his voice.

She lifted her head and looked at him, a question amidst the tears in her eyes. "What are you talking about?"

Jay took a deep breath before answering her. "I'm the one who told Antoine about the affair. A friend of mine saw you there with Mario and she told me. I didn't tell Antoine right off; instead I checked it out for myself and I saw you at The Plaza—you and Mario. That's when I told him and I wish now I wouldn't have," Jay concluded. He didn't mention his cousin's name, not wanting to drag her into the drama.

They sat in silence for several minutes; the only audible signs being their rhythmic breathing and India's sniffles. Jay wanted to say more but not knowing how she was going to eventually react to what he'd already told her, he decided against it. He waited patiently for the verdict.

Finally, India spoke. "I could easily be angry with you, Jay. I could pretend the whole thing is your fault, but the truth is it's my fault. You wouldn't have seen me there had I not been there, and had you not told Antoine and he somehow found out you knew, that would have jeopardized your friendship."

Jay finally released the deep breath he'd been holding since she began speaking. "Still, I just hate seeing you two like this. I hate that I said–"

India interjected. "Maya would have done the same thing. I appreciate your honesty, but let's not waste another minute talking about it. You came here to see Antoine," rising to her feet she concluded, "and it's time for me to go home and try to get a good night's sleep."

Hugging her, Jay said, "I'm gonna keep talking to him. He's stubborn as all get out, but I won't stop until I talk some sense into his head."

"I appreciate it," India said. She retrieved her purse from the chair next to the one she'd just vacated. Going home wasn't what she wanted to do, but there was no sense in spending another night in the hospital's lobby.

"Be careful," Jay cautioned as she headed toward the entrance.

Nodding she turned, tears in her eyes, she replied, "Tell him I'll never stop loving him. Never."

Chapter 40

Shifting uncomfortably in the small, compact car, he peered through the rearview mirror, patiently waiting for her exit. The Dodge Caliber was too small to accommodate his long limbs, but it would have to suffice. The police were looking for him and he had to remain inconspicuous. All he needed before leaving town was her, and once he had her he'd disappear forever, without a trace.

India wiped her tears away with the back of her hands. She'd been waiting all day to see Antoine but still he refused to allow her visits. How could she blame him though? No matter what words of comfort Beverly and Jay offered, India knew it was her actions that led to him being shot. He could have died and she'd have no one to blame but herself. Walking with her head down, she fumbled through her purse.

He sat erect in the small car when he saw her, his head nearly touching the top. Finally, she had emerged from the hospital's main entrance and was now only a few feet away from him, heading toward her car. Careful not to alarm, he quickly slid back down, reclining the bucket seat as far back as it would go. He listened to the click-clack of her heels against the pavement, bringing her closer and closer.

A few feet from her vehicle, India used her car's remote entry to pop the locks. She exhaled a deep sigh, unable to hide her disappointment. She had no idea what her plans were for tonight. Her mother fussed about her staying at home alone. Cassandra feared the deranged man would come back for India. Cassandra didn't want India to be alone, but India was convinced that Mario had fled the country. There was no way he'd risk being caught and locked away. She was sure he was long gone by now.

Mario heard her walk past his car. *Click-clack, click-clack.* He'd parked just two rows behind her. He quickly exited from the car's rear.

Just as India reached for her door's handle, she heard him, but it was too late to get away. He grabbed her from behind before she was able to turn around. She kicked wildly, unable to move her arms because he had them pinned against her.

He had to act quickly before someone saw them. He removed the white, linen handkerchief from his pocket and pressed it over her mouth and nose. The strange scent stung her nostrils, causing her eyes to water. She kept trying to fight for her freedom but soon her limbs ceased to cooperate. He drug her limp body to the passenger side of her vehicle, opened the door, and deposited her body into the leather seat. He quickly hurried back to the driver's side of the car, retrieved her keys from her purse, and started the engine on the baby blue BMW. Mario took a final look around the dark parking lot. Satisfied that no one had witnessed the scene, he sped away, disappearing into the night.

"Finally, Sharon, we can be together again," he whispered as he used his right hand to caress her cheek while guiding the steering wheel with his left hand.

Chapter 41

After the phone call
As we continued to travel, I paid close attention to my surroundings, casually talking to Mario about the different cities we were passing through. I hoped like hell that my phone line was still open. I kept hoping to hear sirens in the distance, closing in on my car, coming to rescue me from Cujo.

"Baby, how much longer we got to ride? I really need to go to the little girl's room," I told him, rubbing his arm with my soft fingertips.

"We'll be there soon, Sharon. Just hold tight."

If only I could get him to pull over. That way I could get to a phone, a police officer, or someone who could get me away from him. I had to do something because I had no idea what he might do once we arrived at our final destination. *Final destination,* I dreaded the thought.

"Baby, can you pull over at the next gas station or restaurant? I can't hold it much longer," I whined, still stroking his arm.

"Look, Sharon, I'm glad to have you back with me, but I have to be real careful right now," he said, taking is eyes off the road to stare into my eyes. "I must warn you, if you try to get away from me, things are going to get real ugly, real fast. Please, don't force my hand."

Staring back into his green eyes made my body tremble with fear. For the first time since I'd met him, I noticed just how cold his eyes were. There was no soul behind them; his eyes were a window to the gates of hell. Suddenly I was too afraid to plan my big escape. My only hope was that my mother and the police were tracing the call and would get to me before it was too late.

Chapter 42

Cassandra and the officers were indeed tracing the call. She cringed when she heard that man threaten her daughter. *Things are going to get real ugly, real fast,* she'd heard him say. She covered her mouth to stifle the cry that danced on the tip of her tongue. A police officer made eye contact with her and firmly pressed his finger to his thin lips, warning her to remain quiet. They couldn't risk Mario hearing their voices through India's open phone line.

Feeling helpless and defeated, Cassandra excused herself from the house. She needed air, so she retreated to her front porch. Outside, she released her fearful screams and moans as tears spilled from her eyes. She had no idea what Mario was capable of, but the police assured her they would catch him and bring India home safely. They were putting out bulletins all over the state of Alabama as well as Mississippi and Louisiana being they were heading west. They'd also learned that Mario's birth place was a small city on the bayou, Chalmette, Louisiana.

Watching the clouds in the sky drift by effortlessly, Cassandra realized she hadn't called Antoine nor Maya to let them know about India's kidnapping. Trey was with Maya's family, enjoying the company of her three sons. He didn't have a clue what was going on with his mother and Cassandra didn't know where to begin in telling him. Maybe it was best that she said nothing; after all, he was only nine.

Ric and his family were vacationing in Hawaii. She thought of calling him but didn't want to interrupt his vacation. Knowing Ric he'd be on the first thing smoking and that wife of his would be boiling like a pot of water with smoke steaming from her ears. Sonya was surely a piece of work and though Cassandra would have preferred Maya to be her daughter-in-law, she did her best to make Sonya feel like a part of their family—that's when she graced them with her presence.

Cassandra glanced downward at the wristwatch that adorned her left wrist; it was still early. She doubted Antoine had been released. Rather than calling him she decided it best to tell him in person before he saw it on the news. She let the officer in charge know where she was headed and assured them she'd return shortly. She didn't worry as she drove away in her pearl white Jaguar; if she couldn't trust her home to the police, who could she trust it to?

When she entered Antoine's room, the doctor was on his way out. Judging by the smile on Antoine's face, he was getting ready to go home. His best friend, Jay sat at his bedside.

"Cassandra, how are you?" Antoine asked his mother-in-law. Jay stood and embraced her. Both Antoine and Jay took note of the somber expression on her face. They could easily see that something was bothering her.

"Antoine," she began as she reached out for his hand, "he's got India. Mario has my baby." As soon as the words escaped her lips, she broke down into hysterical sobs. Jay caught her quivering body before she collapsed to the floor.

Looking up at Antoine, Jay recognized the look in his friend's eyes. He was ready to go after Mario and put him out of their lives once and for all.

Chapter 43

Maya could barely understand a word as Cassandra shrilled hastily into the receiver. She understood that Mario had India and Antoine and Jay were going after them.

"What can I do, Ms. Cassandra? What can I do?" she asked hopelessly. Maya stood at the kitchen window watching her sons and Trey play in the backyard. Tony was schooling them in a game of basketball, four on one. They were all laughing, obviously enjoying their Sunday morning activities. The thought of Trey's mother, her best friend, in danger brought tears down her cheeks.

"Don't tell Trey...not yet. I don't want to upset him. Let's just pray, Maya. Let's just pray that the police or Antoine and Jay find her before...before...oh my God," she cried, "what if he kills my baby?"

Maya told Cassandra she was on her way; Tony was more than capable of taking care of the boys. After she disconnected the call, she stepped to the back door and called Tony aside. She put on a happy face in front of the boys, not wanting to cause alarm, but Tony saw through the façade and immediately asked what was troubling her.

"It's India. That guy she was seeing has kidnapped her and Ms. Cassandra is falling apart. I'm going over to do whatever I can do," she confided in her husband as she choked back tears. Thoughts of people hanging from the ceiling and Mario's cold stare filled her mind.

"What about Antoine? Is he still in the hospital? Does he know?" Concern shone through Tony's eyes. India was like family to him and even though he, like Maya, disapproved of her affair, he didn't want any harm to come to her. He'd go after Mario himself if he had to.

"He and Jay are going after them." She explained, as best she could, her broken conversation with Cassandra. "Police all over Alabama, Mississippi, and Louisiana,should be looking for them and India's car."

"What can I do?" Tony was ready to call Antoine and Jay, hoping they'd take him with them. With Antoine fresh out the hospital, they could use him as reinforcement dealing with someone as crazy as Mario Thomas.

Maya pecked her husband on the cheek. "Just take care of the boys, Tony. Don't tell Trey what's going on."

For a moment she contemplated telling him about the letter she received from her aunt. She did call Aunt Shelly, but she hadn't mentioned a word to anyone, other than her mother, as to what they talked about.

"I love you," Tony declared as his wife headed inside to retrieve her purse and keys.

"I love you, too." She smiled lovingly before closing the door.

Will he still love me when I finally come clean and tell the truth? As she drove to Cassandra's, rather than worrying over her own troubles, Maya focused on the more critical matter at hand—India.

Chapter 44

India kept up her act, pretending to be what Mario wanted, his dead wife. Even though she was trying to make conversation with him, she noticed he was peculiarly quiet. He hardly acknowledged her as he drove the car, constantly looking back in the rearview mirror.

He maneuvered the small car into a McDonald's parking lot next to an Enterprise Car Rentals. India sat motionlessly as the car came to a halt in a parking space between a red Dodge Ram pickup and an older white van. She had thoughts of jumping out the car, running and screaming to the top of her lungs for help, but his words still rang fresh in her mind. *Things are going to get real ugly, real fast.*

Mario silenced the engine, removed his seatbelt and turned to face the woman he loved.

"Take your seatbelt off, Sharon. We're going to grab a bite to eat." He leaned in closer to her and pressed his dry lips against hers. His stale breath made her nauseous. "Remember what I said, Sharon. Don't try anything because I don't want to hurt you." He caressed her cheeks with his fingertips as he stared at her, his eyes cold as steel.

India nodded, letting him know she understood completely. He escorted her inside where she used the restroom while he waited outside the door, next to the restaurant's payphone. To the diners in the restaurant, they looked like an average couple who'd been traveling. Their expensive looking clothes were wrinkled from hours of travel and the man looked exhausted, as if he hadn't slept in days.

After ordering their food to go, Mario and India headed back to the parking lot, but instead of re-entering her car, they walked to Enterprise Car Rentals. Mario knew by now that India's family knew she was missing and the police would soon be searching for her car. No one knew where they were headed, but he still had to use caution. They were so close to their destination; the last thing he needed was a high-speed chase with the police.

While India stood by quietly, Mario secured a car. Rather than using a credit card, he paid the young man a large sum of cash and gave him a fake name. The teen's smile stretched a mile; it was obvious he'd never seen so much cash in his life—at least not cash he could claim as his own.

"There's more where that came from, Ronnie," Mario assured him. "When I return this car in a few days, I'll bring the other half to you. All you have to do is keep your mouth closed."

Ronnie eagerly agreed, nodding his head and saying, "Yes, Sir" repeatedly.

India's hopes of being rescued dwindled as they pulled out the parking lot and continued their journey west to a destination unbeknownst to her.

Her cell phone and purse remained in her car which meant her family and the police could no longer track them. She had no idea when they'd stop again and even if they did, she doubted she'd have the nerve to try to escape. She truly feared that no matter how much Mario claimed to love her—or Sharon rather—he'd kill her if she tried to escape.

A long line of police cruisers whizzed by them at high speeds, lights flashing and sirens wailing. Mario peered through the rearview mirror, watching as the cars turned into the McDonald's parking lot where they'd abandoned the blue BMW. *How in the hell did they find us?* he wondered. He'd been with her every second since they left the hospital. She couldn't have called the police from McDonald's because he waited at the pay phone. There was no one else in there; he'd checked before allowing her to go inside. The stalls had been empty.

Turning to her, Mario voiced his thoughts. "How in the hell did they find us?"

Frightened, India shrugged her shoulders like a child caught with dirty hands in the cookie jar. "I don't know, honey. I... you...you know I didn't call anyone. You were right there with me."

Mario hadn't thought about her cell phone, not until that moment. "Where is it, Sharon?" he asked, anger simmering.

"Where is what?" She saw the fire in his eyes and contemplated jumping out the speeding car. Being that Mario was driving sixty miles an hour, she doubted she'd survive her dramatic exit. The thought of her bones breaking as her body collided with the pavement made her teeth rattle.

"The phone! Give me your cell phone now," he yelled.

"I don't have it." She shook her head from side to side, patting herself down to prove her point. "It's in the car, in my purse. I didn't even have it turned on. You know you can't use cell phones in the hospital," she stammered. Her heart was racing faster than the accelerating Stratus.

Mario peered back through the rearview once again, half expecting to see blue lights closing in on them. He'd paid the kid well for the car rental and to keep his mouth closed. If that punk ratted him out he'd choke his tongue out his mouth.

He didn't know how the police found them; he didn't have his cell phone turned on so they couldn't be tracking him. He'd used cash every time they stopped. How they found them was a mystery, but he believed Sharon. She couldn't have had the cell phone on. Surely it would have been ringing off the hook, calls from her family wanting to know of her whereabouts. Not once had it rang, not one single time.

"I'm sorry," he apologized. "I should have known better. Can you forgive me?"

She nodded affirmatively, offering him a nervous smile. Her heart continued to pound, causing a stinging pain within her chest walls. Mario still wondered how the police had located them, but he was sure of one thing; it wasn't because of anything Sharon did.

Chapter 45

"They found the car," Cassandra yelled into the phone. Antoine relayed the information to Jay as they sped through Columbus, GA, quickly approaching the Alabama state line.

"Is India okay? Is she alright?" Antoine asked his mother-in-law. "Where did they find the car?"

"Hold on one second, Antoine. The Meridian Police in Mississippi have the car surrounded at McDonalds." Cassandra paused, waiting to hear further from the officer in charge.

The older officer's eyebrows raised in question as he made eye contact with Cassandra. Into the mouthpiece, he asked, "Are you sure they're not there?"

Cassandra's heart dropped and again she nearly crashed to the floor. One of the officers caught her in his arms as Maya took the phone from her hands.

"Antoine, it's Maya. The police found the car but no sign of India or Mario so far." Her eyes filled with tears as Cassandra's painful screams filled the house, bouncing from wall to wall. As the officer relayed more info so did Maya. "The cell phone was found under the seat in her car, along with her purse. It doesn't appear that Mario knows she was able to make the call to her mother. People in the restaurant remember them coming in but none of them seem to know how they left. The police are now checking at the car rental place next to the restaurant."

"Damn it!" Antoine slammed his fist into the glove compartment causing it to fly open. He told Jay what Maya had told him. "But we do know he's from Chalmette, Louisiana, right? And it looks like that's what they're headed," Antoine confirmed.

"That's what the police believe." Maya sighed deeply. "But Antoine, you guys are so far behind them. You'll never catch them by car."

That much was true; they were hours away from Louisiana, and even if Jay continued to drive like a bat out of hell without stopping or being stopped by the police, there was no way they'd catch Mario. By the time he reached India, his wife could be dead and Mario could be on his way to God only knows where.

"Give Cassandra my word that we will find India. I'm bringing my wife back sound and safe, Maya. Count on it," Antoine said before ending the call. He quickly dialed his mother's number and filled her in on everything that was happening.

"Is there anything I can do?" Beverly asked. The thought of India being in danger caused her heart to flutter, skipping a few beats as she choked back tears. Antoine assured her that he and Jay would find India but based on what little she had been told about Mario Thomas, Beverly couldn't help but worry. She believed in her son, but the situation was beyond his control; she had to go to God.

"Be careful my son," she whispered. After hanging up the phone, Beverly retreated to her bedroom, closed and locked the door, and fell to her knees. "Father in Heaven," she began as tears raced down her mocha chocolate face.

Maya did her best to console Cassandra, but after the police officers spoke with the car rental clerk who advised he hadn't seen the couple, they were back at square one. All they had was a strong hunch that Mario was en route to Louisiana, but they had no clue as to how he was traveling there. They didn't even know if he and India were still alive. As far as they could tell the two of them had magically vanished into thin air. With that report, Cassandra's hope of being reunited with India also vanished into that same thin air.

"We'll never catch them by car," Antoine said, staring out the window at the WELCOME TO ALABAMA sign they passed.

Jay looked to Antoine for guidance. "What now?"

Without answering, Antoine opened his phone and began dialing a series of numbers. When a female voice answered, he looked at Jay and spoke into the phone's mouthpiece, "I need to know when the next flight leaves for any place close to Chalmette, Louisiana. I need to be on a plane as soon as possible. It's a matter of life and death ."

Chapter 46

As Mario slowed down, turning off the main road, I looked around for landmarks, anything that could help me tell someone just where the hell I was if I was able to get to a phone. I wondered if he still had his cell phone on him; I hadn't seen it.

"Here we are," he announced, stopping in front of a run-down shack. It didn't look as if anybody lived there—ever. The grass and shrubbery were nearly as tall as the house itself and the windows were covered in thick layers of dust. The house looked as if it would come tumbling down right before my eyes at any second.

"Where are we?" I asked, tearing my eyes away from the horrific view and looking to him for an answer.

Mario smiled, removed his seatbelt, and opened the driver's door. "We're home," he announced before stepping out the car.

Home? My mind wondered. Mario opened the passenger side car door for me, extending his right hand. If only I wasn't so frightened of him, I would have taken that opportunity to kick him hard between his legs and make a run for it. But where was I running to? I had no idea where we were and once we turned off the main road we drove a few miles down a road where there were deserted, abandoned houses much like the one he just referred to as home. There was no one to help me.

As we drew closer to the front door of the shack, I realized the house was on water. The wooden walkway creaked under our weight and I feared falling into the muddy water. I was sure it was inhabited by snakes and alligators waiting to eat us alive. Goose bumps covered my arms and I felt my palms become clammy, but Mario didn't seem to notice as he held my left hand in his. He smiled while humming a vaguely familiar childhood lullaby.

The inside of the house was far worse than the outside. A stale fishy stench greeted us as soon as the door opened. I quickly covered my nose and mouth with my free hand as my eyes adjusted to the darkness and dust. Sheets, once white but now a dingy beige, covered furniture. I heard rodents scurry across the wooden floor while spiders climbed the walls, their webs visibly spread throughout the room.

"Why are we here?" I croaked. Dust got trapped in my airway as soon as I opened my mouth to speak; a coughing spell followed on the heels of my question.

"This is home, Sharon." Mario turned to face me, still smiling. "I know we have a lot of work to do, but this is our home now. We're going to raise our kids here. I can teach them how to fish, the way my father taught me, and you dear can teach our girls how to cook fish and make quilts."

Mario pulled me deeper into the heart of what I presumed to be the living room. It was then that I noticed the chalk outlines on the floor. *Oh my God!* A tiny scream escaped and Mario turned to me, staring at me in question. His eyes followed mine to the dust covered outlines on the old wooden floor.

"It's okay. That was years ago, Sharon. It all happened before I met you, and I'm all better now. Your love cured me. I don't hear those voices in my head anymore, telling me to do evil things."

I trembled like a leaf on a tree as he continued to tell me, in no certain terms, just how crazy he was. He put his arms around my waist and stared deeply into my fear-filled eyes. "I love you. I will never hurt you. I'm not that young man anymore."

"Wh…what happened? What did the voices tell you to do, Mario?" my voice trembled as I asked the question. I felt like I was in the middle of a horror film, about to become the final victim before the credits rolled.

"It was so long ago. I was just a teenager, not quite eighteen." His eyes filled with tears and pain. "I don't know what went wrong. I told my parents I'd been having bad headaches and hearing strange voices, but they didn't believe me or simply didn't know how to help me. My mother prayed over me and my father disciplined me, hoping to beat the evil spirits out me." I watched his lips quiver as he spoke. A single tear fell from his right eye and for a second, I felt compassion for him. "I tried to fight the voices; I tried so hard not to give into what they were saying. They kept telling me that my family was evil and they wanted me dead, so I had to kill them. I was so scared because the voices told me if I didn't kill my family, they'd kill me. So, I did it." In detail he told me how he used chloroform to render his family unconscious and how he hanged them, one by one—his mother, father, and younger brother. He then ran to a neighbor's house, a mile or so down the road, and told the man he'd come home and found his family hanging from the ceiling. No one ever suspected him as the killer because he'd always been a well-mannered young man, a student who excelled academically.

"I didn't want to kill them, Sharon. I swear, I didn't want to." He sobbed. "I loved them and I thought I would never experience love again—until I met you. You cured me. I was fine until, until you died, but you're back now. I'm so glad you're back." He squeezed me so tightly I could hardly breathe. "I need you. I need you to keep the voices away, Sharon."

My eyes filled with tears and my heart ached for him, but I still knew he was dangerous. I was no cure for schizophrenia. As soon as the voices overpowered him, I was sure to be killed, hanging from the same ceiling he'd hung his family from roughly twenty years earlier. I didn't know what I had to do, but I knew I had to do something, fast.

Chapter 47

Ronnie breathed a sigh of relief when the police cruisers left. They'd questioned him for over an hour about that man and woman who left in the Dodge Stratus, one of their newer cars on the lot. It was so new that it was not yet registered in the system, and it would take some doing for them to track the car back to their company.

He smiled as he counted the crisp one hundred dollar bills, all twenty-five of them. He'd never seen that much money at one time in his life. There was no way he was turning the man in. The guy promised to not only return the car, but to give him an additional twenty-five hundred dollars for keeping quiet. Ronnie couldn't turn that kind of money down; he planned on using it to venture outside of Mississippi. The world had more to offer than the city of Meridian where he'd spent his eighteen years of life.

"Win the lottery, kid?" Ronnie looked up to see a short, round faced detective approaching him. He'd been so busy counting his loot that he didn't hear the front door chime when the officer entered the business dressed in a fading navy suit and a dingy white shirt with a black tie. He wore a brimmed hat upon his round head and a smile that said, *Gotcha!*

"Yeah, yes, Sir, I scratched off on a jumbo ticket," the teen lied.

The detective smiled, showing his coffee-stained teeth. He extended his hand across the cashier's counter. "I'm Detective David West of the Meridian Police Department. I got a few questions for you, Mr. Lucky," he said, that eerie smile never fading. "I want you to think real hard before you answer me because one wrong answer could land you in the slammer. You understand?" Ronnie nodded slowly as sweat poured from his brow. "Good. Now just where did you come by that money?"

"Sir, I told you—" Detective West held up his right hand, silencing Ronnie before he could incriminate himself any further. "I like you kid, so I'll give you one more chance to tell me the truth." Staring directly into the teen's deep brown eyes, the detective repeated his question, "Where did you come by that money?"

"I, well, Sir—" Ronnie was sweating bullets and his bladder was about to explode. "A guy, the guy the officers asked me about was here. He gave me this money for a car," the young man confessed.

Leaning across the counter, Detective West grabbed Ronnie by his collar. The stench of his Marlboro-Folgers breath filled the teen's nostrils as he spoke. "Do you realize that man is a dangerous lunatic? He kidnapped that woman and because of you she could be dead by now. I got a good mind to place you under arrest and throw away the goddamned key. Now what kind of car did they leave in and which way did they go?"

Hot urine trickled down Ronnie's pant legs as he answered the older man. He told him everything, about the car, the money, and the man's promise to bring more money when he returned the car.

Armed with new information, David called headquarters and gave them the update they desperately needed to find and hopefully rescue India Joiner before it was too late. The rescue mission could quickly become a recovery mission if they didn't find the woman in time.

"You're under police surveillance and therefore ordered not to leave this county," he said pointing his finger at Ronnie. "And if anything happens to that woman, I mean if one hair on her head is out of place, you'll regret the day your father was born."

Detective West confiscated Ronnie's hush money and exited as quietly as he'd entered.

Chapter 48

As soon as they exited the plane, Antoine's phone rang. It was Maya.

"They're in a gray Dodge Stratus," she said as soon as he answered the phone. "A Detective West got the clerk at that Enterprise place to come clean. Where are you guys?"

Looking around at his new surroundings, Antoine answered, "We just got off the plane in New Orleans. We're going to rent a car and track Mario down."

"Maybe you should go to the police and let them know who you are. They should know how to find Mario. Someone around there remembers him, I'm sure," Maya said. She was so happy they were getting closer to finding her best friend. Ms. Cassandra was calm again; she and Antoine's mother had been on the phone praying for hours.

"Maybe, but right now I'm just gonna ask around. The police should've been on top of this all along. If they know where Mario grew up, they should have staked out there hours ago. I'm sure he's made it to his destination by now," he said. Jay was securing a rental car while Antoine continued his phone conversation with Maya.

"Whatever you do, Antoine, be careful. Make sure all three of you come back in one piece."

Inside the rented G-8, the two men buckled their seatbelts. Jay had no idea where they were going so again he turned to Antoine for answers. "Where to?" he asked as he turned the key, bringing the engine to life on the black beauty.

"Let's go to Chalmette, stop at a few stores and ask around. You still got that picture of Mario from the newspaper?" Antoine replied as they coasted toward the main highway.

"Yeah," Jay replied, entering the main highway, heading to Chalmette.

They stopped at some local restaurants but no one knew Mario Thomas. They hadn't seen him, India, or the car the two men described. Antoine thought of calling the police, but if they knew any more than he knew at that point, his wife would be safe. It was obvious they didn't take his wife's safety as seriously as he did.

Jay spotted a small mom and pop store on their right and turned into the small parking area. An older gentleman was behind the counter. Even though it was a hot afternoon day, the store had no air conditioning, only a small mechanical fan on the counter, circulating the hot, stale air throughout the store.

"Afternoon, gentlemen," he greeted them. "Y'all don't look like y'alls from 'round here," he noted as he stared from one to the other.

He was an older man, probably closing in on seventy golden years of life. Though he was tall, his posture was slumping, probably due to arthritis of some sort. What hair he had left to cover his scalp was gray and his smile revealed the vacancy of many teeth.

Jay pulled the newspaper clipping from his wallet and placed it down on the wooden counter. "Do you know this man, Sir?" he asked the older gentleman.

Glasses hung from a chain around the man's neck. He pulled them up to his face before picking up the paper and taking a closer look. "I do declare," he said, still looking at the picture of Mario. "If my eyes don't deceive me, dis here is Ezra and Annie Thomas' boy, Mario. He de only one survived when his family got murdered 'bout twenty years back."

Jay and Antoine looked at each other before turning their attention back to the store owner. "Sir, have you seen this man today?" Antoine asked, his heart beating rapidly. He pulled India's picture from his wallet. "Or this woman?"

"She's a pretty young thang," the old man remarked with a sly grin. "But no, Sir, ain't seen neither of dem 'round here today." He removed the glasses from his face, allowing them to once again dangle from the chain around his neck. "Is dere some kind of trouble?"

Antoine decided against going into details; time was of the essence. "Can you tell us how to get to the Thomas house? We think Mario may be there and it's important that we find him."

"Mario was always a good kid, but dere was something peculiar 'bout him. Everyone believed him when he said he went home and found his folks in dere strung up from de ceiling. De whole town embraced him and saw to it dat he went off to a fine college so he'd never have to look back." The man took a handkerchief from his pocket and rubbed sweat from his face. "But me, I thinks he did it. Dat boy just wasn't right in de head."

"Can you tell me where the house is, Sir?" Antoine asked again.

The man gave them directions to the house and added, "But nobody lives in dat old run down shack anymore. De house been abandoned since de murders."

"Thank you for your help, Mister," Jay said hurriedly, handing the man a twenty dollar bill. Antoine was already out the store and racing toward the car. "Do me one more favor, if you will. Call the police and an ambulance and have them respond to the Thomas house."

"What for?" he asked but to no avail. Jay was already in the car turning the key.

"Yes, 911, dis here is Aaron Taylor. I got two out-of-towners in a black car headed to de old Thomas house on Ferry Landing. I don't know what's 'bout to go down, but dey asked for de police and de ambulance to meet dem dere."

Chapter 49

Mario found candles and decided to light them as soon as the sun set on the bayou. The old house needed a lot of work, and he was determined to start on it first thing in the morning. Due to rodents scurrying about, he decided it best, for Sharon's sake, that they sleep in the car for the night. He didn't want to unnerve her any more than he already had.

She was the first and only person he'd ever confided in about his family's murder. He almost blabbed it to Dr. Martin, but thank God the voices warned him not to. He shouldn't have been seeing a shrink anyway. If it wasn't for that lying bitch, Angela, claiming he'd become obsessed with her, he never would have been made to seek therapy. His job, however, threatened to fire him if he didn't get the help they thought he needed.

The voices told him to kill Angela but lucky for her, she left town long before he stopped seeing Dr. Martin. The doctor prescribed him medication for depression, saying that the death of his wife had brought on unimaginable stress that his mind had not been able to cope with. According to the good doctor, when Mario started dating Angela he wanted so badly for her to be Sharon that he became obsessed with her, calling her by his wife's name. The young woman even claimed he tried to abduct her after she broke up with him.

He stared toward the window. How anyone could believe he thought that lying bitch was Sharon was a mystery to him. She was nothing like Sharon. Sharon was an honorable, beautiful woman, so unlike Angela. She was a cheap whore just looking to get laid by any man who gave her the time of day.

India sat restlessly in a wooden chair near a raised window. The heat was stifling and her clothes were drenched in perspiration. Her mouth was dry as cotton, but they had no water or food. Mario promised they'd go to the store once the sun set; a part of her wanted to just die of dehydration. She'd given up any hope of being found.

If only she'd remained faithful to her marital vows, none of this would be happening. She'd be at home with her husband and their kids rather than stuck in the swamp with a psychotic murderer.

She thought of her son, never seeing him again and grief filled her heart. She'd never see him graduate high school or college. He'd get married some day, but she wouldn't be there. And Ariel, they'd just repaired their relationship and now she was being ripped away from her as well.

Her fear soon turned into anger as tears continued to saturate her perspiring face. Anger turned to rage and before she was fully aware of her actions, she was on her feet glaring at Mario.

"I want to go home," she demanded, her teeth clenched tightly and her hands resting at her sides in balled fists.

"Sharon, we are home," he said as he scurried across the floor toward her.

"I am not Sharon!" she screamed at the top of her lungs. "I am not your wife, Mario. Sharon is dead. She's gone and she's not coming back. I am not your wife." At that point she didn't care what happened next. She was tired, fed up with being away from her loved ones and fed up with being afraid. If she was going to die, she was going to die fighting.

As he approached her, she began swinging her arms wildly, landing several blows into his chest and face. "Calm down, baby. Calm down," he whispered as he fought desperately to restrain her.

"No! No!" she screamed, breaking away from him. She made a beeline for the front door which stood open. The wooden walkway creaked, threatening to give way under her weight, as she ran toward the car.

Knowing he had the keys, she didn't stop at the car. She ran as fast as she could down the deserted road that led to the main highway. Through sweat and tears, she saw a black car fastly approaching. Waving her arms as she continued to sprint, she yelled, "Help! Help!"

Mario noticed the black car, too. He stopped running, pulled his gun from his pocket and fired once, hoping to regain control of the situation. India fell to the ground right in the path of the oncoming vehicle.

Chapter 50

Jay hit the brakes, bringing the car to an abrupt stop a few feet away from India's body. Both car doors flew open and the men made a hasty exit. They heard the distinct sound of police sirens in the distance.

"India," Antoine yelled as he scooped his wife up into his arms and scurried to the back of the car. "Baby, are you okay? India!"

Mario cursed to himself when he saw who exited the car. He walked slowly toward the car, determined to finish Antoine off. He wouldn't shoot him anywhere except his head this time. He would make sure that son-of-a-bitch didn't come after him a second time.

"You just couldn't leave us alone, could you?" he yelled. "Now, look what you've made me do to her!" Tears filled his eyes and his voice quivered. Hurting Sharon was the last thing he'd wanted to do, but because of Antoine's interference he'd had no other choice.

Antoine pulled his own weapon from his waistband. He was sure to come prepared for battle and he sure as hell didn't bring a knife to a gunfight. He checked the magazine clip and snapped it back into place before peeping from the rear of the car. He saw Mario approaching, his gun already drawn as tears drenched his twisted face.

Mario fired a few shots at Antoine before the man ducked back behind the car. "You shouldn't have come here," he yelled. "You should have just left us alone. She's my wife!" Another loud explosion rang from the gun, releasing yet another bullet with Antoine's name on it.

Just as he reached the front of the car, Mario observed police cruisers swiftly approaching. He turned abruptly, running back toward the old house. Antoine stood, raised his gun and aimed it at his target. He squeezed one eye shut and fingered the trigger, but just before he snapped it back, releasing a single bullet that would end their living nightmare, Jay grabbed his hand.

"Let the police handle it, Ant," Jay pleaded. "Besides, you're not the kind of man that shoots another man in the back. That's a coward, and I know you better than that."

The police shot by as Antoine, reluctantly, surrendered his gun to Jay. He fell to his knees at his wife's side, ignoring his own pain. Jay flagged down the ambulance and two EMTs scurried out the vehicle, coming to India's aide. Antoine prayed they weren't too late.

Mario barricaded himself inside the shack. He only had one bullet left and there was no way he could kill all the officers he observed from the front window.

A tall black officer took a bullhorn from one of the cruisers. "We have the house surrounded. Come out with your hands up, or we'll be forced to come in by any means necessary," he warned in a gruff voice.

Mario, his belly to the floor, scurried to the rear of the house, where he slowly and cautiously lifted his head and peeked out the window. Sure enough a group of officers were gathering across the bayou. Even if he escaped, he'd have to stay in the water for hours or even days before they gave up the search for him.

He returned to the front window to negotiate with the officers. "Send in my wife!"

"Sir, your wife is dead. Come out or we'll be forced to come in!" the officer in charge reiterated.

Dead? He didn't mean to kill her; he just wanted to scare her. He fired the gun to scare Sharon, not to kill her. The last thing he wanted to do was kill her. Tears slid down his face as he contemplated his next move.

A sharp pain ambushed his cranium and the voices started talking to him, telling him to point the gun to his head and blow his brains out.

"No," he yelled to the voices. "No. Leave me alone. I won't. I won't do it!"

"Do it," they antagonized. *"Do it! She's dead now, you can't control us. Go ahead, make my day!"* They laughed, imitating Clint Eastwood.

"Stop it! Stop it!" Mario cried, scurrying into a corner like a small child. The gun slipped from his hands and fell to the floor. Closing his eyes, he curled his knees to his chest and cried like he was having a bad dream. Repeatedly he clapped his open hands over his ears, trying to drown out the evil voices. "Stop it! Leave me alone! I'm not listening to you! Sharon, help me! Help me!"

The officers listened to his psychotic breakdown from outside. Chief Rouse, the man in charge, shook his head in disbelief. Initially, when they were contacted about the kidnapping, he shrugged it off as non-urgent. To him it sounded like a woman running off with her lover; for all he knew the two of them had planned to get rid of the husband and live happily ever after. He wasn't going to send his officers out to look for the lovebirds. But when the call came in from a citizen requesting police and ambulance, he quickly assembled personnel and rushed to the scene. His gut told him that something was terribly wrong and his first instinct had been wrong.

Taking a deep breath, realizing he couldn't undo his mistake, the gray-headed police chief gave the signal for his officers to go inside and subdue the suspect. He hung his head in shame. Had he acted when first contacted, just maybe things would have turned out differently.

"I always knew you'd come back." Mario's eyes flew open at the sound of his mother's sweet voice. Standing before him was the family he killed all those years ago. They hadn't aged one day. *"It's not your fault, my son. You told us you needed help, but we didn't want to believe you were sick. It's not your fault."*

He remembered that day. The voices were yelling at him to kill his family. His first victim was his brother, Johnny. Johnny had been five years younger than Mario, not quite a teenager at the time of his death. Mario found him lying across his bed studying. He took a handkerchief doused with chloroform and held it to the youth's nose until he was unconscious.

He then wandered into the kitchen where his mother was cooking their supper. He hugged her from behind before using the same handkerchief to render her unconscious. Ten minutes later, his father finally came home from fishing on the bayou.

"Help me clean the fish, Son," his father called from the back door.

Still under the guidance of the voices, Mario rushed his father, knocking him off his feet. He quickly covered his face with the chloroform-doused handkerchief, pressing it against his nostrils until he lay still. One by one, he hanged them, his mother last. He wanted to kill none of them but especially not his mother. He loved her most of all. He remembered how her green eyes flew open as she hung lifelessly from the ceiling.

Slowly rising to his feet, Mario walked toward his family. All three were dressed in the same clothing they'd been wearing the day he murdered them. Just as he reached out to hug his mother, they all vanished.

"Momma!" he cried before he was tackled to the worn, dusty wooden floor by two officers. "Momma!"

Chapter 51

"It's over! It's finally over!" Antoine cried breathlessly into the phone.

Cassandra jumped for joy, praising God with every leap.

Maya picked up the phone which was now lying on the floor as Ms. Cassandra continued her praise dance.

"How is she? Is she okay?" Maya asked Antoine.

"Why don't I let you ask her," he said, handing the phone to his wife.

"Maya," India exclaimed. "Oh, Maya!"

When the bullet breezed by her ear, India had fallen to the ground and fainted. The ambulance took her to the hospital to hydrate and examine her. She was assured that Mario was going to be locked away for a long time and would likely spend the rest of his life in a mental institution. Antoine would have rather seen the man dead, but he was satisfied with the outcome.

"I was so scared, India. Thank God you're okay! I can't wait to see you." Tears of joy flooded Maya's face at the sound of India's voice. Her friend was alive; she was okay.

After talking to Maya and her mother a few minutes longer, making sure the kids were okay, India ended the call. She turned to Antoine and said, "I'm so sorry for getting us into this-this mess. If I could–"

He silenced her with a tender kiss. "It's over, baby. Let's put it all behind us and just go home." And together, along with Jay, they boarded a plane, Georgia-bound.

Chapter 52

To say that I was lucky would be an understatement. I was blessed in spite of my infidelity. God definitely had his arms of love and protection around me. He replaced my fear with enough anger and determination to run for freedom on that fateful day rather than lying down to die by Mario's hands.

Mario received the maximum sentence and we were assured he'd never see the light of day again. A part of me felt badly for him; had his parents gotten him the help he needed as a teenager maybe they'd still be alive and he could've had a normal life. Instead he allowed himself to believe his one great love was his cure and when he lost her, his mind couldn't accept that so he obsessed over innocent women, hoping they could bring his mind the calmness it experienced with her.

Antoine made a complete recovery physically and emotionally. I thank God the police showed up when they did; I fear what would have happened had Antoine and Mario had a shootout. My husband would likely be serving time now for murder or worse. He could have been murdered; just a matter of who was quicker to the draw. That thought sickens me to my stomach many days.

Our kids don't know about my affair or the abduction; all they know is that we're finally a happy family. They're excited about the bulge in my belly. Ariel is hoping for a girl and Trey has his heart set on a boy. Antoine and I just pray to God for a healthy baby; one who will love us despite our flaws and imperfections. We're still learning and know all will be well as long as we have love and faith.

Antoine was so happy when we found out I was pregnant. That news couldn't have come at a better time for us. I felt our reunion was solidified with the pending birth of our child.

Rachel, Annette, and Lisa haven't changed but what matters is that I no longer empower them to change me. There are moments when their words fly out Ariel's mouth, but I've learned to be patient, taking the time to teach her better. When she blossoms into a young woman, she'll carry those lessons with her into adulthood. I pray that I can lead by example and be a positive role model for my kids.

Dr. Martin, Mario's former shrink, introduced himself to us one Sunday after church. Momma invited him back to her place for a family dinner and wouldn't you know he and Momma began dating? After losing the love of her life, Momma finally decided to date again. Dr. Martin seems like a great guy; she says he's a keeper.

Maya invited me to lunch today. She said she's got something very important to share with me. I can't imagine what it is being that we never keep secrets from each other. There's nothing she doesn't know about me and nothing I don't know about her. We're thick as thieves; two peas in a pod.

"Hey you," she said as she sat across from me. Casually dressed in a mid-sleeve green shirt and jeans, she looked beautiful as always. The green shirt highlighted the green specks in her hazel eyes. Her long, silky bob rested on her shoulders and her skin was glowing as usual.

"Hey yourself," I replied with a bright smile.

"So, how was your doctor's visit today? Is our little girl still kicking up a storm or what?" She, like Ariel, was rooting for a girl. She even went as far as to pick out a name for the baby, Mayanna, after her of course. It was cool though, I liked the name and who better to name my child after than her godmother?

I filled her in on the doctor's visit after we placed our order and waited for our food. As we sipped the chilled lemonade, we talked about my return to work and how good it felt to be back in my office doing what I loved. With Mario out the picture, Antoine had no coils about me going back to work. Teresa and the rest of the staff welcomed me back with open arms. Of course there was gossip about Mario and me but it was to be expected. I didn't let it define me or interfere with my work; I still hold it down on the second floor.

"So, what's up?" I asked after the idle chitchat ended. I was dying to know what she had to tell me. Finally, we could stop talking about me and my drama. I'd die happy if I never heard the name Mario Thomas again.

"There's something I need to tell you. It's something very important and I need you to promise that you won't be angry at me. Just try to understand the explanation I give." Tears filled her eyes and my heart raced. I didn't like where our conversation was headed. For Maya to be afraid of me becoming angry, the news had to be bad.

I leaned across the table as far as I could before my precious cargo was pressed against it. I took Maya's hands in mine. "There's nothing you can tell me that will make me angry. I love you. We've been through thick and thin, girl. Nothing can change how I feel about you. You know that."

Maya closed her eyes and sighed deeply, slowly inhaling and then exhaling. "I have a daughter. Her name is Camille."

I opened my mouth to ask when and how since I'd known her since we were in high school, but she shushed me and continued.

"Camille is Ric's daughter, India. When I moved to Chicago with my grandmother, I was four months pregnant. I had the baby, but—"

"Does he know? Does my brother know he has a daughter?" I asked, flabbergasted. I felt as though the wind had been knocked out of my sails and I was just drifting along. Looking at the woman sitting across from me, I no longer recognized her as the best friend I'd grown up with. My best friend never would have kept something so vital from me or Ric. She was a complete stranger to me.

Maya shook her head; Ric didn't know. My brother had a child in the world that he didn't know about. How could Maya keep that from him? What kind of woman did that?

I couldn't mask the anger I felt. "How could you?" I asked, pounding my fist into the table, causing our beverages to spill. People stared intently at us, but I didn't care.

"India, just give me a chance to explain," she begged, doing her best to clean up the mess I'd made.

"All these years, Maya. All these years, I've looked up to you like you were some kind of saint, some kind of Mother Theresa, and all this time you've been lying to me, to Ric even by not telling him about his daughter! Does Tony know?" The look on her face spoke volumes; he didn't.

The server came over and tried to clean up the spill on the table, but I angrily shooed him away. I didn't appreciate the unwelcomed interruption. This conversation was between Maya and me, one that was way past due.

"India, if you'll just calm down, I'll explain," she tried to reason. She tried to place her hands over mine, but I quickly snatched them away. I didn't want to feel the touch of a stranger.

I gathered my purse and rose from the table. I couldn't bear the sight of her any longer; she suddenly repulsed me. The woman I idolized and dreamed of becoming was now flawed.

"India," she yelled behind me. When I stopped and spun around, she hurried to face me.

"Is my secret so different from yours? Did you tell your husband you may be carrying Mario's baby?" she hissed. I could tell by the look on her face that she regretted the words as soon as they shot out her mouth like a ball from a cannon, but it was too late to take them back.

Her words cut like a knife, deep and to the core. Only she knew my examination at the Chalmette Medical Center revealed I'd been raped during the abduction. Apparently while I was in the car, out cold, Mario had his way with me, without using a condom. I begged the hospital staff not to reveal that information to anyone, not even the police. I didn't want my husband to know; didn't want him to ever think I could be pregnant from Mario.

Antoine said the past was behind us and we should focus on moving on. I was happy to have my husband back and there was no way I was going to tell him I could possibly be carrying Mario's child when it was equally possible that the child I carried was indeed his. I prayed day and night that our child was not the offspring of Mario Thomas, the conception of a silent rape.

"Fuck you, Maya," I spat before stomping out the restaurant.

I heard her calling behind me, but her words fell upon deaf ears. As far as I was concerned, the friendship was over and Maya Jefferson was dead to me.

Here's a sneak preview of
What's a Wife to Do?
by Linda R. Herman

Available 2010 in paperback from
Xpress Yourself Publishing

Derek

I arrived at Piedmont Academy at one forty-five. Just as I approached Tia in the lobby, I heard a familiar voice call my name. I turned to see my wife standing a few feet away and nearly wet myself. Had Tia really make good on her little threat?

Elise was dressed in a baby blue pant suit; her long hair pinned up. Her eyes were hidden behind a pair of dark shades. The day I'd avoided for five years had finally arrived. I knew I'd have to face the truth one day but I wasn't expecting it to happen today.

My heart dropped to my feet. "Elise?" I barely whispered her name.

Waving a bottle of water, Elise said, "Honey, you don't look so good. You need a sip of my water?"

Feeling sick, I looked from Tia to Elise-Elise to Tia. The look of fear etched into Tia's face proved that she wasn't expecting to see Elise any more than I was.

Removing her shades and brushing past me, Elise approached Tia. "Tia?" she confirmed, extending her right hand.

Tia stuttered, "Hel-lo."

Elise threw her head back and laughed. "Girl, you are not shy! Were you this quiet when you were sleeping with my husband? And the letter you wrote demanding more money didn't sound like you were shy and timid at all. I'm sure you know who I am, right?"

The letter! Elise found the letter in the toolbox. I was sure she found Terrica's picture as well. I should have left all of it at my office. *How could I be so stupid?* What was I thinking? No wonder she was acting so strangely this morning. She knew about Terrica and Tia!

Tia shook her head yes and the rest of her body swayed like a tree in the midst of a hurricane. After all her threats to tell Elise, now that the cat was out the bag, she was more afraid than me.

"Elise, let's go home and talk about this. Let me explain." I tried to usher her outside, not wanting her to create a scene right there in the auditorium.

Elise snatched away, drew her right arm back and slamdunked it into the side of my face. Without blinking she lunged toward Tia who quickly backed away, scurrying into the nearest corner. For the people in the auditorium, the scene before them was much like an episode of Jerry Springer; only they had free tickets and there was no Steve there to stop the fight.

Before Elise could reach Tia, I picked her up and carried her outside hoping that none of her church members or my coworkers were in attendance, witnessing the near fight. My wife was well-respected and loved in our small community and I didn't want her image tainted.

Here's a sneak preview of
In His Father's Arms
by Linda R. Herman

Available 2010 in paperback from
Xpress Yourself Publishing

Simone

"You look beautiful."

He embraced me and it felt so damn good that I toyed with the idea of clearing the table and making myself the entrée, Simone a' la mode. I felt eyes burning the back of my neck and turned slightly, noticing a group of women staring us down. They were no doubt whispering about our hug that had wavered beyond friendly. Reluctantly, yet tactfully, I was the one to end our embrace, all the while smiling facetiously at our shamelessly, gawking audience. I bet every one of those holier than thou sluts wanted a piece of the dark man who whispered naughty words in my ear, making me giggle like a school girl.

My companion pulled out my chair and we ordered our drinks. I was on fire and in need of a Strawberry margarita stat. He ordered rum and coke. We passed on appetizers.

"I'm not a man to beat around the bush." His words were clearly spoken, concise and to the point. "There is a strong attraction between us." I couldn't argue with that. I was feeling him so badly that even my lower lips were smiling. "The only question is what are we going to do about it?"

My pulse rate increased to well over one-hundred as he covered my trembling hand with his. I felt beads of sweat on the back of my neck and my mouth salivated. This man had me so hot and bothered I had to cross my legs for fear that my overheated lust would ooze right out of my pants. If he licked his lips one more time, like LL, I was going to take him in the bathroom and do some naughty things.

Through eyes filled with lust, I stared at the well-built man before me, devouring him with my eyes. His eyes were a deep brown and so dreamy that I lost touch with reality when I stared into them. His eyebrows were thick and his smooth mahogany skin had to taste as sweet as Hershey's chocolate. That long, pink tongue of his was stroking his full lips while he stared at me daringly. To hell with the weave queens who were still watching us like hawks, I was about to pounce on him. The waiter came right on time.

Sitting our drinks on the table, the young man took pen to pad and asked, "May I take your lunch orders?" He focused his attention on me first.

I wanted to tell him to bring on the strawberries and whip cream because the chocolate was already sitting across the table ready to be dipped into my eagerly awaiting mouth. I wanted to lick him from head to toe before mounting his face and showering him with my naturally sweet juices.

LINDA R. HERMAN

LINDA R. HERMAN is the author of *Consequences: When Love Is Blind, Consequences, Somebody Prayed For Me,* and eBooks: *Chemistry 101, From Hooker to Housewife, A Time For Love, Lying to Myself, Single Again. She resides in Georgia with her husband and two children.*

Xpress Yourself Publishing
A Publisher of Fine Books
and
2008 AALAS Independent Publishing
House of the Year

Visit us online:
www.xpressyourselfpublishing.org